HAIR HAT

HAIR HAT

CARRIE SNYDER

PENGUIN
CANADA

PENGUIN CANADA
Penguin Group (Canada), a division of Pearson Penguin Canada Inc.,
10 Alcorn Avenue, Toronto, Ontario M4V 3B2

Penguin Group (U.K.), 80 Strand, London WC2R 0RL, England
Penguin Group (U.S.), 375 Hudson Street, New York, New York 10014, U.S.A.
Penguin Group (Australia) Inc., 250 Camberwell Road, Camberwell, Victoria 3124, Australia
Penguin Group (Ireland), 25 St. Stephen's Green, Dublin 2, Ireland
Penguin Books India (P) Ltd, 11, Community Centre, Panchsheel Park,
New Delhi – 110 017, India
Penguin Group (New Zealand), cnr Rosedale and Airborne Roads, Albany, Auckland 1310,
New Zealand
Penguin Books (South Africa) (Pty) Ltd, 24 Sturdee Avenue, Rosebank 2196, South Africa

Penguin Group, Registered Offices: 80 Strand, London WC2R 0RL, England

First published 2004

(WEB) 10 9 8 7 6 5 4 3 2 1

The support of the Ontario Arts Council during the writing of this book is gratefully acknowledged.

Manufactured in Canada.

NATIONAL LIBRARY OF CANADA CATALOGUING IN PUBLICATION

Snyder, Carrie
Hair hat / Carrie Snyder.

ISBN 0-14-301537-0

I. Title.

PS8587.N785H34 2003 C813'.6 C2003-906529-4

Visit the Penguin Group (Canada) website at **www.penguin.ca**

FOR LINDA AND ARNOLD

When I consider how my light is spent,
Ere half my days, in this dark world and wide,
And that one talent which is death to hide,
Lodged with me useless, though my soul more bent
To serve therewith my Master, and present
My true account, lest he returning chide;
"Doth God exact day-labor, light denied?"
I fondly ask; but Patience to prevent
That murmur, soon replies, "God doth not need
Either man's work or his own gifts; who best
Bear his mild yoke, they serve him best. His state
Is kingly. Thousands at his bidding speed
And post o'er land and ocean without rest:
They also serve who only stand and wait."

—John Milton
"When I Consider How My Light Is Spent," 1673

Contents

YELLOW CHERRIES

I WOKE UP SCREAMING bloody murder. The white numbers on the clock radio beside my head were 3:58. The problem wasn't the scream, it was who had heard the scream.

"Francie?" said the voice beside me, a girl's voice.

I could not tell where I was. The room was very dark, but it had the feeling of a big room. The scream echoed to the high ceiling and fell back on me.

2 HAIR HAT

"Wake up," said the voice, and something pounced on my chest.

"I'm awake," I said.

"Why did you scream?"

"I don't know."

"Girls?" There was a figure at the bedroom door, puffy and glowing white. "Who was screaming?"

"Francie had a bad dream," said the voice on top of me.

"What's happening?" said another voice from across the room, the squeaky voice of another girl in another bed.

"Francie, come to the bathroom," said the glowing white figure, floating quickly across the room. "Come to the bathroom with me." She pulled back the sheet and touched my forehead with the palm of her hand. I was clammy and sweating. "Do you feel sick?"

"No."

"You're hot."

"I feel cold."

"Come to the bathroom." The hallway was so dark you could not see in front of your face. Aunt Lucy steered me with hands on my shoulders, forward, then a sharp turn, then another. The bathroom light came on with a flicker that made me feel sick, three bare bulbs above a rusty mirror in a space as wide as a closet. There was the flat red rug on the floor in front of the sink.

"Do you feel sick?" Aunt Lucy pressed my forehead again. Her nightgown was old-fashioned and sleeveless, with lace at the neck and hem. It was pretty. "Was it a bad dream?"

I nodded. It was better to pretend.

She flipped open the mirrored cabinet, stuck a thermometer under my tongue. "Wait here."

I could not see all the way to the mirror unless I stood on tiptoes, and then could see just the top of my head, with its brown hair cut into heavy bangs and feathered over the ears. I loved the haircut. Nobody wore braids.

The place where I got my braids cut off was air-conditioned, and at first the cold air felt so good. I even said it out loud: "This feels good." Then I started to shiver. On the floor under the chair was all my hair, which the lady kept sweeping into a bigger pile. My mother sat and looked at a magazine with her feet far apart until the lady said, "All done." It cost eight dollars, and I could not stop looking at myself in the mirrors and then, when we walked down the street, in the store windows.

"I miss the braids," said my mother. She was giant beside me, her stomach like a watermelon. The baby was not even due for another month. My face looked small in the store windows under all that hair, and white. It was a very hot day. My mother had two half moons under her armpits. Although I would not say so, the hair brushing all over my face made me feel even hotter.

"Here's a glass of water," said Aunt Lucy, swinging the door shut behind her. The bathroom was warm. It had no air. I was wearing a long T-shirt that flapped to my knees. She read the thermometer while I sipped at the glass. "You're fine," she said.

I sipped some more water.

"Do you have to pee?" she said, and left me alone again. I could hear her breathing outside in the hallway. "Back to bed," she said when she heard the toilet flush. She watched me wash my hands. I felt alone and very small. It was a feeling like being lost.

I had the same feeling when I went with my best friend into the woods, once, behind her parents' cottage, and we went past a thousand pine trees, until everything was very quiet and we could not see the sky.

"Let's go back," I said, and we turned around and walked and walked, until we knew we had walked too far.

"We're walking in circles," said my best friend.

I thought we'd seen that clump of brambles before. "We should go that way," I said.

But she didn't remember the brambles. She started to scream, "Help! Help!"

"Shut up," I said. "That's not going to help," and then I started to scream too.

We stopped screaming and looked at each other, walked some more, and started screaming again. We could not help it. The screams bubbled up.

My best friend's dad found us. We were not far from the cottage, and he said he could hear us screaming all over the lake. He made cocoa with marshmallows on the gas stove and said not to tell my mother. We were weak and limp and we laughed a lot.

I felt limp inside now, and empty, not like laughing. Aunt Lucy took the glass of water.

"Can I call my mom?" I said.

"We don't want to worry your mother over nothing," said Aunt Lucy. She switched off the bathroom light and steered me back to the bedroom. A fan buzzed in the corner. I could see it in my head: big, square, refrigerator green, sitting on the bare boards of the floor in front of the closet.

Nearest the fan slept Mary on the fold-out cot. We could hear the breath snorting in and out of her nose. She had allergies. Aunt Lucy walked me toward the white numbers of the clock radio and tucked me under the sheet. "Sleep well." She pressed a kiss on my forehead, but it was not the same as my mother's kiss. Aunt Lucy's voice sounded almost like my mother's if I closed my eyes and imagined hard, but she was not my mother.

Katie rolled away from me as the mattress sagged beneath us. The sheets were soft and smelled like lemon detergent. Everything at Aunt Lucy's smelled like this, even the air. I knew exactly where I was now, and exactly how the room looked. I was sharing the double bed with Katie, my cousin, who was two years and nine months older than me. This was her bed, and also Mary's bed. Mary got the cot when I was visiting because of her allergies, and Katie said she'd rather sleep with me because I didn't kick. There was a yellow fluffy rug on the floor and yellow paint on the walls and a strip of Holly Hobby paper running around the middle of the wall like a belt. The clock made a clicking noise when the numbers flipped over: 4:27, 4:28. Katie sighed and thrashed her arm around, smashing me in the ear. I could see why Mary kicked.

It seemed the light had gone pink outside the windows, and just then the room turned chilly. I wished I had more than a sheet covering me.

~

"You were screaming and screaming," said Katie, gobbling up a bowl of cornflakes. She tried to pour herself a second helping, but Aunt Lucy grabbed the box. "But I'm still hungry," said Katie.

"Have a drink of juice, then," said Aunt Lucy.

"Juice isn't filling."

"Wait for the eggs."

Katie was jammed into a pair of tight blue shorts. She had the beginnings of breasts. Last night, she told Mary and me what they felt like: they hurt and tingled. Mary said she didn't want them anyway. Katie said, "No, but it's not a bad hurt. It's a good hurt." That didn't make sense. Katie rolled over. "You wouldn't understand." No more questions.

On the grey table, Aunt Lucy had set out bright-coloured plastic bowls, a pitcher of orange juice, a white jug holding a plastic bag of milk with wet drops on its sides, and the box of cornflakes, no-name brand. She was frying scrambled eggs too, and sausage, at the stove behind where Katie sat.

"Mary, you're too little for that. She's too little for that, Mom," said Steph, who was the oldest. She was buttering the toast. Mary poured milk over the top of her glass and onto the table. It ran in a river down the centre and dripped through a crack to the floor. "I told you," said Steph. "I told her."

"Clean that up, Steph," said Aunt Lucy, looking over her shoulder at me. "Why aren't you finishing your cereal, Francie?"

"Why should I have to clean it up?"

"Are you talking back, young lady?"

I pushed the flakes around the bowl with my spoon. They were soggy and almost colourless in the sea of milk. The kitchen was noisy and busy and hot, and I did not want to eat. Steph stuck her long blond hair behind her perfect ears and made grown-up clucking sounds with her tongue as she wiped the table clean, then knelt and crawled under to wipe the floor. Mary sipped milk from the top of the glass without lifting it and kicked her chair leg.

"Aren't you hungry, Francie?" said Aunt Lucy. The eggs were done, and Uncle Marvin appeared and sat at the table too. He had summers off from teaching school. He spent the days outside, busy with a small red tractor, a riding lawn mower, a silver pickup truck. He had a moustache and a fat round face, like a boy's.

"What's on the menu, Lucy?" he said.

Aunt Lucy spooned eggs onto a plate, and three sausages, and Steph ran over with two slices of freshly buttered toast. "It's just out of the toaster, Dad," she said.

"Why so stingy with the sausage?" Uncle Marvin said to Aunt Lucy.

She served eggs and sausage to Katie and Mary and Steph. "You have to finish your cereal first," she told me, but I couldn't. Aunt Lucy did not sit at the table. She stood by the sink and drank a cup of coffee. She had a red bathrobe over her nightgown, and her hair was a mess.

Uncle Marvin smelled minty and soapy. He was sitting next to me. His hair was still wet, lying flat against his head. I looked at his hands. The backs were tanned, with small blond hairs on the knuckles. They gripped the fork and knife and ripped the sausages apart, shovelled eggs onto toast. He ate until there was just a crust of toast left, placed the knife and fork crosswise on the plate, and pushed back his chair.

The kitchen had gone quiet while he was eating. Everyone else was eating too. I tried, but the cornflakes melted in my mouth and gagged me.

"Busy day," said Uncle Marvin. "See you at lunchtime."

The screen door shut with a swat, and we heard a motor starting up.

The dog barked. I did not like the dog one bit. It was an outdoor dog, part German shepherd, scruffy at the shoulders. Sometimes it was on a chain by the barn, barking and barking, but other times Uncle Marvin let it run free.

Yesterday, after Mom and Dad drove away, I was walking to the barn with Mary to look at her pony and the dog burst out of the corn, mouth wide open, heading straight for me. I ran to the house, but not fast enough. The dog snapped and bit me on the leg. Aunt Lucy yelled at Uncle Marvin, but he said, "If she didn't run, he wouldn't chase her."

"It's only a little bite," said Aunt Lucy, sitting me on the kitchen chair and pulling my shorts up to take a better look. "No blood." She swabbed it with iodine, which turned my leg brown.

"Can I call my mom?" I said.

"They won't be home yet. We won't bother her with this." Aunt Lucy gave me a sugar cookie, homemade and very soft, but my stomach still felt empty after I ate it.

This morning, Aunt Lucy looked out the window over the sink and said, "The dog's all tied up today, Francie. No need to worry."

The girls carried their dishes to the counter. Steph washed and Katie dried. Mary didn't have to do anything. Neither did I. I was a guest. Mary was too little.

"Today you're picking cherries, girls," said Aunt Lucy. She had run upstairs and back down again, and was wearing a blue summer dress with white flowers sprinkled on it.

"That's a pretty dress," I said. Now that everything was cleared off the table and all the food out of sight, I felt hungry. I opened the fridge door a crack and Aunt Lucy said, "No snacks. We'll have nice bologna sandwiches and potato salad for lunch."

~

The cherry trees were all in a clump beside the field of soybeans. The cherries were yellow. Mary and I ate some. Katie told us not to, then she ate some too. Steph told her not to.

Uncle Marvin rode by on his lawn mower, spitting cut grass that stuck to our feet and legs. He pulled the steering wheel and the mower turned at Mary and me. Mary did not move. It seemed he would run over us. My legs were moving, but my feet slipped and I crashed into the grass. I knew what my face looked like at that moment, the mouth in a stupid O, and I wished I could undo it and throw that face away. Uncle Marvin whirled away at the last second, laughing from inside his throat.

"Don't you scare those girls," shouted Aunt Lucy, sticking her head out the screen door. The lawn mower roared, and it looked like Uncle Marvin had not heard. He chewed on a blade of grass, long and feathered at the end, as he drove away from us all, toward the barn.

"You should have seen your face," said Katie.

I didn't look at her. I brushed grass off my stomach and ate another cherry.

"She's doing it again," said Katie to Steph, and Steph said, "Leave her alone. You know what Mom said."

"My friend died," I said.

"We know," said Katie.

"Shut up," said Steph.

"She fell in the creek and drowned," I said. When I said this to grown-ups, their faces changed, their cheeks sucked in. The sound of their voices lifted, softened, spread out wide. They said, "Poor, poor girl," meaning me, maybe, or maybe meaning my best friend. It did not matter; either way, I was included. My cousins were not like grown-ups.

"Did you get to see her drowned?" said Katie. "I heard their faces get all purple."

"I'll tell Mom," said Steph.

Katie popped a cherry in her mouth and leaned into my face. "Did you?" she whispered. Her breath was hot and stinky under the smell of yellow cherry. The smell of yellow cherry is not like the smell of red cherry. It is like something kept in a box for a while.

"No," I said.

"They probably had a closed coffin," said Steph. Her cardboard basket was almost full.

"What do you know about it?" said Katie.

Steph shrugged. "We're not supposed to talk about it."

"You started it."

Mary looked up at me. I could see right down her pug nose. "Why was she dead?"

"She fell in the creek," I said.

"Why?" said Mary. She was a baby, only five years old.

"I guess she couldn't swim," I said. I hadn't thought of it before: the strange thing was, she *could* swim. We took swimming lessons together and she was twice as good as me. No one had passed the swimming class except for her. We were all jealous, and also of her black bathing suit, which came from a special store. I wasn't jealous of her mother, even though she gave us store-bought powdered donuts out of a plastic tray when I came to play. Her mother wore dark glasses and waited in her air-conditioned car, parked outside the swimming pool fence. All the other mothers sat on the concrete benches and watched, or at least left and then came back at the right time. No one else stayed in a car with the windows rolled up, smoking cigarettes.

"Was she your best friend?" said Mary.

"Yes."

She was my only friend. She had other friends, but I did not, except through her. I did not know why. On the schoolyard at recess, she could play anything she wanted: kiss tag, double rope, truth or dare. If she wanted to jump rope, I could too, but someone always pushed in front of me. If I said, "It's my turn, not yours," nobody seemed to hear. My words floated out and disappeared. Sometimes I wondered whether I'd said them out loud.

Once, my voice cracked and the words came out funny, split open in the middle. Everyone laughed. They heard that time. They tried to make the sound again to laugh some more. My best friend laughed too. I saw her looking at me, not in a mean way. She was not mean. I tried to laugh too, but just then everyone stopped, and it sounded wrong. Ha ha! Ha ha ha!

"You must be sad," said Mary.

"Yes."

"Was she pretty?"

"Yes."

"Do you miss her?"

"Yes."

"Stop asking dumb questions," said Steph. "Francie doesn't want to talk about it."

But I did. I did want to talk. I wanted to tell them what nobody knew: that we were both by the creek, playing, when she fell in. I didn't push her, hardly at all. Why didn't she swim?

~

I ran and ran, but when I got home, I did not know what to say. Mom was sleeping on the couch. Dad's car was gone from the concrete slab out front. It took them two whole days to find her. Mom told me at lunchtime while I ate a peanut butter sandwich.

"Would you like banana on that?" she said.

"Yes," I said.

She cut up a banana with a butter knife and unpasted the slices of bread. It took her forever to lay the banana slices on the bread. Before she handed the sandwich back to me, she said, "Oh, Francie, I don't know how to tell you."

I reached for the sandwich and she let me take it. Her eyes ran with tears. "Your little friend has been found and she is dead."

She wasn't little. She was two heads taller than me, but not fat.

"Oh," I said. I took a bite.

"It's the shock," said my mother. Her face was soaking wet. "It's the shock of it. Imagine."

School had been out for four days then. It was the start of summer holidays. I whispered the words "summer holidays" to myself when the metal doors with the tiny steel-gridded windows opened and we ran down the shady cement steps. The street was warm, almost hot, and I kicked off my shoes. The rule was that you had to wear shoes until summer holidays. Tiny stones hurt my feet. I had to run with my soles all curled in. Summer holidays, I whispered. I could see all those months before me, wide open.

I said the words to myself as I swallowed a bite of sandwich: summer holidays.

"What a tragedy." Mom's nose was red. "Thank God it wasn't you."

Chew, chew, chew, swallow. I ate the whole sandwich. I was still hungry, but Mom sat beside me and held my hand. "You can cry," she said. "Don't be afraid to cry."

"Okay," I said. I did not want to cry. Part of me had wanted her dead, just to see what it felt like. Now I knew. It felt like nothing. I had thought it might be an adventure, but it was not.

My mother rubbed her thumb along the back of my hand and said, "She was a sweet girl, the sweetest. A good girl. So friendly." She rubbed some more, until it hurt. "So young. So very, very young."

Seven years old is not that young. She was almost eight. She was friendly, but she was not sweet. She had a way of asking about things that were none of her business. "Where is your Dad?" she would say to me when she spent the night. "Where's Mr. Vittari?" she once said to Mom. Mom's face turned in on itself and she said, "Mind your own business, Nosy Parker."

"Don't speak ill of the dead," said Mom when I reminded her.

"But you remember, don't you? You remember?"

Mom did not say anything. She was not looking at me. She was shaking her head sadly, not crying any more. Sighing as she looked at the tabletop and swept a few crumbs into her hand.

~

"This is a nice basket of cherries," said Aunt Lucy. "You did a good job."

The others lined their baskets up on the counter too. Aunt Lucy dumped each into the sink and began picking off stems and digging out pits. The pits and stems went into a white plastic bucket with a metal handle. They would go on the compost pile.

"Go outside and play," said Aunt Lucy. Her hands flashed. She had a special tool for pulling the pits out. Syrup boiled on the stove.

We were in the barn when we heard the dog barking. Mary's little pony kicked her hoof and trotted away from us, out into the small field of grass behind the barn. Her stall opened onto it, and she was free to come and go. If it rained, she could come inside. Mary never rode her. The pony was pretty and grey, but not very nice. She once kicked Mary in the leg, and then she kicked Uncle Marvin too when he came to see what was wrong. I wished I had seen that.

The dog was barking its head off, growling and snapping. Mary stuck her head out of the big sliding barn door. I looked over her shoulder. The dog was pulling on the end of its chain as if it might rip through its collar.

A man with a hat stood at the back door. He had a briefcase in one hand. His small white car sat blocking the lane. Aunt Lucy stood half in and half out of the doorway. We could see her dress with the white flowers blowing around her shins. The man with the hat had on a dark suit. The dog strained and growled. Aunt Lucy shook her head and her hands. She waved her hands like she was waving away a fly, then a bigger fly, then a whole bunch of flies.

"Go away," she said. We could hear her all the way from the barn.

"What's this?" said Uncle Marvin, puttering up on his tractor. He parked by the dog and reached down, patted its straining, ugly head. "I don't like the looks of this."

In a flash, the dog was off the chain. Uncle Marvin had set it loose.

The man with the hat turned and saw the dog. I knew exactly how he felt. His legs danced under him as he leaped for the car, yanking on the door in a panic. His hat never moved. The dog had its teeth into his pant leg, and we saw a rip just before the door opened and the man hopped inside, throwing his suitcase into the back. The door slammed. The dog jumped up to the open window, and we saw the man's elbow pumping like crazy to raise it. The dog jumped and jumped.

It took the man forever to drive up to the barn and turn around. I saw his face up close, quite red, and his tall hat brushing the roof as he reversed, pulled on the steering wheel, drove forward, reversed again. The dog ran along beside him, picking up speed all the way down the lane.

Uncle Marvin laughed. Aunt Lucy was not there any more. She had shut the door and gone inside. She did not want to see it. The dog ran back up the lane and Uncle Marvin patted its head.

"Good girl," he said. "Lousy salesmen." He hopped on his tractor and drove into the back fields. The dog followed. It was loose again, and I was in the barn, a long way from the house.

"Don't be scared," said Mary.

"I'm not."

"Are you hungry?"

"No."

"That dog never bit me," said Mary. "You have to walk."

We walked. Mary held my hand. I hated her for it.

"You made it just fine," said Aunt Lucy. She had eight jars packed with cherries sitting on the counter by the sink, and she was pouring in syrup with a ladle.

“I’m hungry,” said Mary.

“You can wait another half an hour,” said Aunt Lucy.

“I can’t,” said Mary.

“I have a surprise for you,” said Aunt Lucy.

“For me?” said Mary.

“No, for Francie. Francie’s got a new baby sister.”

“Already?”

“Isn’t that good news.”

“Yes,” I said.

“Your father called just after you went to the barn. Isn’t that exciting?” She put the ladle back into the pot of syrup and got two cookies out of the cookie jar. It was a green metal tin with silver cursive letters that said “Cookies.”

We ate the cookies sitting on baby chairs in the front room. It was hot with no windows open. The chairs were shaped like a panda and a red bear. I had the red bear. It had ears at the top and the fur was matted down. “You’re too big for that chair,” said Mary. “You’re squashing it down.”

Cookie crumbs fell on my lap, onto my bare legs.

“How long are you going to stay?” said Mary.

I pushed the crumbs off with my hand. My legs felt funny. I could see all the little white hairs on them. I did not look at Mary.

“Are you sad for your friend?” she said.

If I held absolutely still, I could pretend she wasn't there. There was a rushing noise in my head. Everything in me stayed perfectly quiet. I did not know why. Mary stood in front of me. Her eyes were two inches from my eyes. "What's the matter?" she said. Then she left. I did not move. Maybe I did not even breathe. I could hear Mary in the kitchen, telling on me. The chair was squashed under me, almost squashed right to the floor and tipping over. I had to press my heels down hard to keep from falling off. The air was very hot and my new haircut itched my face.

I had sat in this chair forever, for as long as I could remember. This was the first time it was too small. The red bear chair had always been my favourite, always. I knew what it meant to be sad: the chair was too small. Still, I would not cry. I did not even want to cry.

I just wanted to hold absolutely still.

TUMBLEWEED

"GET OUT OF THE CAR, PLEASE," I said to Edwin. "Mommy's going to pull out her hair if you don't get out of the car now."

"Yah, Edwin, get a move on," said Georgia. She was hopping from foot to foot on the hot pavement, clutching a wicker bag in both hands. A bottle of lotion fell out of the bag.

"Pick that up, please," I said. "You should have worn sandals. I told you to bring your sandals. What if you step on glass?"

"Whatever," she said, trying to pluck the bottle between her long toes; her father's toes. She also had his long fingers, his baby fine hair, his glowing blue eyes. Of me, she had the ears. Maybe. One can't really tell with ears.

"Use your hands, for heaven's sake," I said.

"Why couldn't Daddy come?" she said. "See, I can get it with my foot."

There came the steady thumping of Edwin's small round heels on the rolled-up window of the back door.

"Daddy had to drive to Toronto to see Grandma," I said. "Grandma couldn't wait another minute to see Daddy, so he had to go."

"I'm ready now," said Georgia, the bottle of lotion raised knee-high. She hopped one step too many, lost her balance, and staggered against me. The bones of her back felt so small, so rigid. "Geez, Mom. Let go already."

Twelve years old. People might be watching.

"Edwin," I said, yanking the door open. "Put your sandals back on. We're here."

"I know," he said.

"All right, then."

"Can I get a hot dog from that man?"

"What man?"

"Like last time."

"This is a different beach. We've never been to this beach," I said. "Don't start wailing."

"Why did we have to bring him?" said Georgia. "He could have gone with Daddy to see Grandma."

"There are bound to be hot dogs here too," I said. "Grandma didn't want to see anyone but Daddy. That's what Daddy said."

"Not even me?" said Georgia.

"I don't know. You'd have to ask your father."

"I hate when you say that."

"Don't make me come in and get you, Edwin," I said. I put my hand around his fat little leg. Edwin kicked. "Young man, I do not have the patience for this."

"Can we go, Mom?" said Georgia.

"Have you put on sunscreen?" I said. "You could do that now. Use the car window as a mirror."

"You already said that," she said.

"When?" I said. "When did I say that?" I buckled one of Edwin's sandals and reached for the other.

"Before we even left." She sighed. She was examining her face in the window, as I'd suggested.

"Up and at 'em." I tugged Edwin upright. "Don't you look adorable." He wore a red sun hat attached under his chin with an elastic band.

"He's old enough to walk on his own," said Georgia. I

put Edwin down. Between his T-shirt and swimming trunks was a soft stripe of tummy.

"You can carry the umbrella," I said to him.

"I don't want to."

"Then I'll carry it," I said, clutching umbrella, cooler, purse, and car keys.

"What do I get to carry?" said Edwin. "I want to carry something."

"Come on," said Georgia, halfway over a dune.

"Wait for us, Georgia," I called as her fair head blinked out of sight. "Why not the umbrella? It's the easiest thing." This was not true; it was cumbersome, and Edwin would look like an ant hauling a toothpick. But I couldn't hand over my purse or the car keys, and the cooler was out of the question.

"So?" said Edwin. "I don't want to."

The skin of his arm was cool under my sweating palm. "We don't want Georgia to get to the beach first, do we? We don't want her to get the best spot." The cooler thumped against my thigh. It was ridiculously oversized for our purposes, but I hadn't been thinking clearly. I had been thinking, Get out of here, hurry, dammit dammit dammit. Three lonely plums rolled about inside, knocking up against a large bottle of tap water, a bag of potato chips, three cheese sandwiches slapped together on white fluff bread and tarted up with the scraps of iceberg lettuce that had not gone completely brown in the crisper.

"Georgia," howled Edwin. "Wait for us."

~

"Go and play." Georgia was already at the water's perimeter. I stabbed the brown-and-white umbrella into the sand and flapped open the Smurf beach towel.

"That's mine," observed Edwin.

"I'm just borrowing it to sit on."

"Where's the shovel?" he said. "Where's the bucket?"

Forgotten, in the mess of our exit. "Put your bathing suits on, children, we're going to the beach." My voice carolling in my ears. "Won't this be fun."

Georgia hadn't wanted to wear her bathing suit under her clothes. "Who was that on the phone?" she asked.

"Nobody," I said. "Nobody. Just someone for your dad."

"That's somebody."

"If you put your bathing suit on now, you won't have to change at the beach."

"You never answer me."

In my head, I answered her. In my head, I said, There are things you do not wish to know, young lady. There are things you should be glad you do not know. That somebody is better as a nobody.

Edwin was waiting. "My shovel?" he said sadly.

"Oh, honey," I said. "I'm so sorry."

"I was going to dig," he said.

We looked until we found a stick in the edges where the sand thinned out and met brambles and grass. There were not swarms of people, as there would have been earlier in the season. It was a weekday in late August, the sky overcast.

Edwin stirred at the sand with his stick. I plucked a sandwich from the cooler and gnawed it, although I was not hungry. It gave me something to do. I never brought a book to the beach, or anything that might distract me from rescuing my children, in leaps and bounds, should the occasion arise.

It was a weekday in late August, I said to myself, as if telling a story, pinning it down. In my mind flashed the picture of a knee uncovered, hairless, pristine, a hand slipping upward. It had been flashing in my mind all morning. *Don't.*

"Georgia," I said, waving as she pretended not to see. A pack of teenage boys dashed into the water near where she was playing, her feet in the shallow froth. "Georgia, don't wander too far, please."

The boys had taken no notice of her, I was relieved to see, standing in her hot pink two-piece, hair plastered to scalp, water washing in over her ankles and back out again. Edwin crouched nearby, stick abandoned, digging a hole with his bare hands. Patties. His hands were not yet hands, were still patties, dimpled at the knuckles and round.

"Are they still patties, Mommy?" he said from time to time, holding them out for inspection.

And they still were. I did not want them to become hands.

"It was a blessing, not an accident," we said, over and over, the year after Edwin was born.

The sandwich had grown limp and pasty. I held onto it without purpose, watching my daughter observe casually the teenage boys leaping like dolphins from the water to catch a Frisbee. She was at once so young and so intent on undoing her youth, unlatching it from about her and throwing it away, growing up. Don't hurry, I wished to tell her. Wait.

The shouts of the boys rose and fell and were infectious.

A young woman was shouting too, clad in a purple bathing suit and spilling out of it in unflattering places as she ran along the beach, flip-flops flapping laboriously. It took a moment to register her cries, her waving arms, to hear them for what they were.

"Help, help!" she called, skidding in the sand.

Edwin and Georgia lifted their heads like daisies to the sun and watched her cut a trail between us.

"Somebody," she called. "Help!"

I laid down the sandwich and rose on my haunches. The woman was fleeing toward the concession booth. It seemed impractical to chase after her.

"Mom," said Georgia, "what did that lady want?"

I came down to them and placed my hand on Edwin's heated hair. We saw the woman slip and fall and a man with a beard bend and pull her up by the elbow. It was at a distance now, and the scene played out silently. Edwin ducked my hand and returned to his hole.

"Look how big, Mommy."

The cries of the teenage boys did not subside. Georgia and I watched the bearded man pull the woman to her feet, watched her point in a direction behind us, watched her crumple against the man in a way that looked intimate and hopeless.

"What is that lady doing, Mom?" said Georgia.

"I don't know," I said.

"She was shouting," said Georgia.

"That man will help her," I said.

He had dropped her on the ground and was running toward us, waving his arms, calling, just as the woman had done. "A man is drowning," we heard as he nipped past us on bare feet. We turned, Georgia and I, and watched him splash into the lake toward a figure we could barely make out, although there was a great deal of turbulence in the water surrounding it. People were beginning to gather. Several more men dashed through the waves and pumped their arms like swimmers in a race.

"Dude, what's going on?" shouted one of the teenage boys, and the Frisbee landed on the water and floated past him and he did not notice.

"Perhaps," I said, "I should just grab my purse, and we'll get some food at the concession stand."

"Okay," said Georgia, looking stiff and uncertain.

"Come with us, Edwin," I said.

"My hole," said Edwin. "I'm not done."

"You can finish it later."

The concession stand, a low wooden-framed structure with a metal awning, was all but deserted. Several used paper napkins with yellow mustard crumples blew lightly across the pavement as we neared. We ordered an extra-large fries to share, and I let Georgia get a cheeseburger and Edwin a hot dog, and we all split a tub-sized Coke.

The young man in the paper hat, who served us through a square window with a screen that drew open and closed, looked over our shoulders as he took our order. "What's going on out there?" he said.

We had taken a circuitous route to avoid the woman in the purple bathing suit, who lay near the water's edge like a giant fish washed up on shore.

"I don't know," I said at the same moment that Georgia said, "Someone's drowning."

"We don't know that, Georgia."

The sirens tolled as we sat at a picnic bench to eat. "If we carry this food all the way back to our towels, it will get cold and sandy," I said.

"What's that noise?" said Edwin.

"It must be an ambulance," I said.

"That man might have died," said Georgia. We looked toward the beach and saw that the woman in the purple bathing suit was gone.

"Why?" said Edwin.

"Georgia," I said.

"Do I have to eat this?" said Edwin, squeezing the tail end of his hot dog.

"Isn't it yummy?" I said. "Georgia, wait for us, please."

"You should have done something." She was perched at the end of the picnic table, ready to fly away.

"It's yuck," said Edwin.

"Don't eat it, then. Put it in the garbage bin."

"You should have done something, you know."

"There's bees on that garbage."

"Give it to me, Edwin."

"Can I get another one?"

"You're not even listening. What do you care."

"Edwin, for pity's sake. Georgia, come back here this minute."

Her limbs had grown so long. From a small distance, she looked like a young lady, marching toward the activity, prepared to be a purposeful bystander.

"Georgia, come back here right now."

"Can I get another, Mommy?"

"No, you may not, young man."

"Why are you yelling?"

"Don't cry," I said. "Georgia, please slow down. Please wait for us."

She was on the Smurf towel, lying on her stomach, head buried in her arms. As we neared, I imagined her face puckered with tears, but she rolled on her side and blinked and I saw that her eyes were dry.

"My hole," said Edwin, running down toward the water, which had advanced on and blotted it out.

"What happened?" I said to Georgia.

"What do you care."

"I do care, honey," I said. "I do."

"I don't know," she said and shrugged.

The water was quiet where all those people had been. The teenage boys were gone, the bearded man, the woman in the purple. A clot of slovenly women and their skinny, scampering children alighted near us with batches of plastic toys and a brown picnic blanket. The women lit cigarettes and shivered as they plopped down to stay. The sky was slate grey and a wind was picking up over the lake.

"I think it's time to go," I said, waving away cigarette smoke. "We've had quite a day."

"When is Daddy getting home?" said Georgia. "Maybe we could go out for supper."

"I don't know," I said.

"We could have Chinese."

"I thought you didn't like Chinese."

"Daddy likes Chinese."

"Yes, he does. That's a nice thought, Georgia. We'll see." I flipped out the Smurf towel and shook sand onto sand. "Put on your sandals, Edwin."

"I don't know where they are."

They were nowhere to be found. We looked behind the umbrella, the cooler, broached the tumbling children along the water's edge, trampling futilely back and forth. Georgia wanted to go all the way to the concession stand, but I couldn't bear the thought. It was such a distance. They were a cheap pair anyway, a gift from his grandmother, a notorious bargain-hunter. The sole of the one had been coming off.

"It's quiet," said Georgia, despite the calling of the gulls. We flung them our cheese sandwiches and watched as the birds ravaged each other to get at them.

"Climb onto my back," I said to Edwin. "I'll carry you to the car." His fat little arms wrapped around my neck, and I was glad for their warmth, for the way they nearly choked me as I gathered umbrella, cooler, purse, and keys, and heaved my way toward the parking lot.

"Mommy!" shouted Georgia, who had run on ahead. Her hands were quivering, I saw, and her legs goose-pimpled under the shorts she'd pulled on to cover her bathing suit. These days, she called me Mom, not Mommy.

It was our car, the driver's-side window smashed in, fragments of hard glass littering the front seats. The CD player had been ripped out, the empty maw of the glove compartment hung open, and in the middle of the back seat, almost mathematically positioned, was a plastic cup half filled with dark liquid.

"Oh, Jesus," I said. "Oh, damn."

"You swore," said Georgia, shocked. "I'm telling Daddy."

"You tell Daddy," I said. "You go right ahead."

"Is he really at Grandma's," she said.

Silence. The several swats of umbrella, cooler, purse, and keys falling to the pavement. The way I wrapped my arms around my daughter and breathed in her hair, my son's arms latched around my neck, warm and smelling of damp and salt and ketchup. "Oh, honey," I said. "Oh, sweetheart. I'm not mad at you."

"I never said that," she said.

"No, you didn't," I said. "I'm sorry."

"It's okay, Mommy," said Edwin, huffing and puffing in my ear.

"Are you crying?" said Georgia. She was steady now and pulling away from me.

"We'll just sweep this glass off the seat and we'll be fine. There wasn't much to take, that's lucky," I said.

"Why would someone do this?" said Georgia, breathless with anger now. "Why?"

"I don't know," I said.

"It's so mean," she said. "I hate them."

"They didn't know it was our car. They weren't thinking about us when they did it."

I thought, He wasn't. He wasn't thinking about us when he did it. It made me feel braver than I had known I could be. I was halfway to feeling elated.

We picked out the larger pieces of glass with our hands, working as a team.

"Don't drink that," I said to Edwin, who was crawling the back seat.

"I know," he said, lifting the cup importantly with both hands and creeping on his bottom to the open door. Coke splashed on the pavement.

"That man has hair like a cowboy hat," said Georgia, whispering at me, pointing. A man in striped bathing trunks was loping across the parking lot. It was a fair distance from him to us, but I saw that Georgia was right: it was not a hat on his head; it was hair grown into the shape of a hat. I felt a strange dread beating inside my stomach.

"Don't point," I said, reaching for her hand. "Don't make a scene."

It was too late. Edwin ran with the plastic cup on bare feet toward the garbage bin, and the man with the hair hat swooped in between him and us like a vulture. From where we were, it looked like the man would intercept Edwin on his way back to the car, pluck my little boy out of reach with his ropy hands, capture my baby in his long, long arms.

"Don't you dare," I screamed, and other things, cruel things, too cruel to recall. The man stopped in bafflement, as did Edwin, both staring at me from across miles of pavement.

"Mom," said Georgia, sinking down in the front seat.

"Edwin," I said and clapped my hands to him, calling him to me. He ran on rounded bare feet, never once touching the bits of broken glass that littered this place, flying over all danger.

"I threw it out by myself," he said as I settled him into the booster chair, snapped the seat belt in place. My face was hot, my mind confused, darkened. I did not look up to see whether the hair hat man was still standing watching us. I did not want to know.

Georgia and I laid towels on our seats to cover the shards that could not be picked up, and I put the car into gear, heading for home.

"He's gone," said Georgia, turning around.

"Good," I said, although that was not what I felt in my heart. In my heart was a great wrenching, as if I were missing the only thing that mattered.

Before we had even reached the main highway, the wind blew riotously through the broken window, keening in our ears.

"Windy!" shouted Edwin in delight, and Georgia shut her eyes to feel more intensely the air brushing her skin.

We were tumbleweed rolling across a prairie field.

A slim and forgotten fragment from my youth opened up and poured over me: curled under a thin bedsheet, reading books about cowboys riding the range. How I had loved the cowboys, their long lonely nights spent outdoors under a stream of stars, their smell of worn leather and horseflesh. In the scorching daylight, tumbleweed rolled over hill and dale, beautiful and terrible both. The sign of something on the loose, something joyful and untameable. The sign of a terrible drought to come. The cowboys would sing of it around the campfire at night.

I looked at my daughter, pale hair lifting and dancing around her skull, and I thought she would understand. If only I could find a way to tell her.

PERSONAL SAFETY DEVICE

"JENNY! JENNY!"

No one called me that any more, except my gran: "Whoops, hon. I know you prefer Jennifer now that you're all grown up."

"Jenny!" The man's walnut-fat face was troublingly familiar. Under other circumstances, I would have let him slip by in a crowd, but there was no crowd, only a scattering of mufflered students, and he was advancing on me like a little engine, steaming over the slabs of stone that marked the middle of campus, a gathering place with concrete vats of flowers in the spring. It was March, too early for flowers, and a skiff of filthy snow adorned everything around us, lumpy reaches of ice awaiting the unsuspecting foot. His boots hit a patch, and he skidded and danced quite daintily for a beaverish fellow.

I placed him.

He had been nameless even then, at a barbeque event in my parents' backyard for my father's slo-pitch team.

I was fourteen, hopeful that handsome sons would be brought along. I mooned about the lilac bush, practising my seductive hair flip and open-mouthed smile with a diminishing hope of return. A handful of little kids beat each other over the head with foam-rubber contraptions. There was just one remotely suitable specimen, a skinny boy with bad posture and an attempt at a moustache.

Not my type, I thought darkly. My type, in theory, rode a motorcycle and was tall, preferably blond, and strikingly handsome. He would sweep down upon me like a storm, and in a deep voice . . . well, I was incapable of filling in the blanks, but the scenario would doubtless end with his fingers brushing the hair off my forehead and his eyes gazing stormily into mine. It would be an all-around storm-ridden event.

"We're off the beer," said a woman tanned like a leather hide. "We only drink the hard stuff these days."

"Better for you," said her husband, slapping his belly grotesquely and swinging a bottle of clear, potent liquid.

"Ha ha ha, now that's a good one!" shouted my father, stabbing the air with barbeque tongs.

"Where's your tonic, dear?" said the woman to my mother, who was downing a plastic tumbler of cheap white wine like there was no tomorrow.

I hated them all, exquisitely.

It was there, by the dying lilac, that this man had discovered me. He had arrived by himself and seemed at the edges of things, having backed so far away from the main group, with their wife-grabbing and liquor-swilling, that he had stumbled into my section of the yard. His glasses magnified two eyes to a preposterous rotundity. He clutched a paper plate with a hot dog and a pile of chips upon it, and stumbled over a clump of geraniums.

I soon learned he was a teetotaller, and soon after learned what teetotaller meant, and before he had even started his hot dog, he announced he was born again. That was enough for me. I'm sure I did not properly excuse myself before wandering up to my bedroom to sulk and write in my journal. You don't want to know what I was writing. In fact, I don't want to know. I have since thrown out the evidence of my wishful, hopeful, all-consuming, incredibly boring search for hot boys.

"Jenny!" he said now, arriving at my elbow and standing a fraction too close. His little mittened hands were clutched together with such excitement and pleasure that I could hardly bear it. "You probably don't remember me."

"No," I said, ruthlessly preparing to retreat. "I'm sorry."

"That's okay. No trouble at all." And he explained about the slo-pitch team, how he had been the manager, not an actual player. "With my stumpy leg, I haven't been able to do everything I wanted. This one is shorter than the other one. But your father was kind enough to bring me on the team."

"I must get to class." I was headed to the on-campus bar for a mid-afternoon drink and to meet a young man from my psych class. The search for hot boys was still on, although the journal entries were better, I thought; made sophisticated by mention of rum & Cokes and cigarettes; made dramatic by complicated triangulations, late-night phone calls, bitter goodbyes.

"Of course, of course," he said. "But before you go, have you given any thought to personal safety devices? They are very important nowadays."

"Personal safety devices?" Surely he wasn't referring to condoms.

"Now, Jenny, before you say anything to the contrary, I must let you know that money won't be a problem. We can arrange a payment plan—only nineteen ninety-five a month. I know you students are on a budget."

"Are you selling something?"

"It comes with its own carrying case, which slips easily into a backpack or purse."

"Huh."

"In fact," he said, oblivious to the cold and to his own running nose, "I've got a wonderful idea. It came to me when I saw you, and I thought, How lucky to have run into someone I know." He beamed like a madman.

"I've really got to get going."

"Jenny, I have been wondering: How best to reach these kids?" He paused for dramatic effect. "Through one of their own, of course. And I'd give you 5 percent commission on all sales."

"You want me to sell this thing?"

"I'd waive the initial upfront fee and give it to you for just nineteen ninety-five a month. Battery pack included, and carrying case, plus the emergency first-aid kit at no extra cost."

"All that and it fits into a purse?"

"It depends on the size of the purse," he said.

"I'm sorry, but I don't think I'm the right person for this." I had been temporarily amused, picturing myself regaling the young man at the bar with a spot-on impression of the encounter, but I had enough material now; too much.

"You wouldn't have to be selling, that's the beauty of it. That's the beauty."

"I'm sorry." I checked my wrist for its non-existent watch.

He was accompanied by a black bag of a size too large to be carried comfortably by the strap. It dragged on the ground as he pursued me. "You could tell people about it when it came up in conversation. All very natural. Jenny, I'll let you in on the offer for just fifteen ninety-five a month. With the battery pack, carrying case, first-aid emergency kit, that's a value of over two hundred dollars."

"Leave me alone, please." I was done with him. I was finished.

"Jenny," he said. "Jenny, did I say something wrong?"

"I'm late." He would have to drop the bag to keep up with me, and he was not willing to do that.

"Thanks for your time," he called. "It was a real pleasure." His head was very round and his ears stuck out at an angle nearly perpendicular beneath a blue toque. I was sorry, to tell the truth. I was sorry to be such a poor substitute for his good idea.

My date was not amused. I fell all over myself to please him, embellishing the event with chirpy alacrity. He stared morosely into his beer. My type had changed. It was now the brooding, slender, sweatered sort with shaggy hair. He would slump in front of me in class and unaccountably address me afterward, all dark eyes and tender sarcasm. Late at night, I would listen to Leonard Cohen and recall this moment until my roommate groaned that she could bear it no longer.

"So," I said, far too sprightly for his liking. "What would you like to do?" He yawned into a clenched fist.

"Oh," he said. "Another beer, maybe."

"Right," I said. "Another beer."

"Have you seen that girl around?" He nodded at a petite young thing in smart black boots and a pixie haircut. Once upon a time, I'd had the misfortune of possessing such a haircut. It made me look like a plumpish adolescent boy. I'd wept for an entire evening, then moped for the next six months as the hair grew through various stages, all agonizingly unflattering. This girl looked like I had imagined I would, delicate and finely cut and fragile as a reed.

"No," I said. "Do you know her?"

"Not really," he said, gazing. She looked up from across the smoky room and straight at us. A smile flickered.

My date sighed and fingered his glass. Perhaps "date" was too strong a term for the occasion. "Do you want to get together sometime?" had been his precise words. Oh yes, I'd bleated. How fun.

"Excuse me for a minute," he said, standing.

Oh wretched, wretched hour, I imagined writing in my journal that evening. Oh bitter, feckless fate.

"He's not worth it," my roommate would say. She would then make me a cup of instant hot chocolate. We would linger over every move, every word, every inference made by this boy, who was now slouching over the pixie girl, holding a fresh pint of beer, smiling benevolently as she fluttered like a little lost bird.

Gag me with a spoon, I thought as she exposed her milky throat to him. Those words had not come to me since childhood, when a friend's sister had said them and we'd all laughed like hyenas at the picture it made. Gag me with a spoon. It was our favourite thing to say for the next few weeks, then it faded into the distance. A new favourite rose to take its place—"grody to the max," or "P-U," or good old, reliable old "barf."

"So," said my date when he'd returned. "See you 'round, then."

We did not run into each other for over a week. I suffered silent agonies; and a few not-so-silent ones. He skipped two psych classes, then turned up at the third and asked to borrow my notes.

"You bet," I said brightly.

"Cool," he said.

Although I did not smoke, I accompanied him outside after class, standing in a late-March gale sucking gamely on one of his high-tar cigarettes.

"Got a light?" said a man with a hat, tapping me on the shoulder.

"Sorry," I said. I'd seen him at the front of our class before, always wearing his hat. It came upon me slowly, from this proximity, that his hat wasn't really a hat. It was made of hair. It was growing from his head. He was too old to be a regular student.

"Here," said the boy I liked, proffering matches.

"Thanks," said the hair hat man, fumbling with them and dropping the packet to the ground, leaning over to pick it up again. "Cold, isn't it."

"Yes," I said. Don't mention hair, I made a mental note. Act normal.

He rubbed his brow, right under the brim. He was having difficulty keeping a match alight. "I just started smoking yesterday, after a few years off."

"Huh," said the boy I liked.

The man's coat pocket bulged. A mechanical hum emanated from within. The hair hat man followed my glance. "Personal safety device," he said, patting the pocket.

"No way," I said.

"You've heard of them, then."

"Sort of."

"Can I have those notes now?" said the boy I liked. "I'm kind of in a hurry."

"Only nineteen ninety-five, plus an entry fee," said the hair hat man.

"Are you some kind of salesman?" said the boy I liked. He was laughing cheekily. I could have smacked him.

"Yes," said the man. "Not a very successful one, I'm afraid." He tipped his hand to the brim of his hat and nodded to us, entirely a gentleman.

"Never mind," I said.

"The notes?" said the boy I liked.

The hair hat man handed the packet of matches back to him, cigarette still unlit. "This wind is too much for me," he said and quietly extricated himself from our company, loping down stone steps, bent and distant.

"Look, I'll get them from someone else if this isn't going to work out," said the boy.

"Did you see his hair?" I said.

"What about it?"

"The hat. His hair was like a hat."

The boy, slowly changing into someone who was not my type, gave me a look. Disgust could be read there, disdain, annoyance. "His hair was a hat," he said, speaking plainly and clearly, as if to a child.

"Wasn't it?"

"I really don't think so," he said.

The cigarette burned itself down to the filter in my bare hands and scorched a finger. I squatted to look through my bag, came up with a fistful of notes and a blank expression. The best I could muster.

"Thanks, doll," he said.

"When can I have those back?" I said. "The final is next week."

"I'll call you," he said.

Yet another event to cart home to the long-suffering roommate. We parsed the use of the term "doll"; presented casually, was it actually semi-hostile, the very opposite of friendly? The "I'll call you" proved quickly to be empty rhetoric, as dismissive and heartbreaking as "See you 'round."

"We could talk about my problems sometimes," said my roommate.

I thought she was joking.

~

The news spread through psych class like the plague. That guy—the one with the sweaters and the shaggy hair, the one who hardly ever came to class—was up on a rape charge.

"I don't believe it," I said. "He has my notes."

"Yah, that's the one," said a weedy-looking kid next to me. "I saw you two together."

"He writes poetry," I said. "I just don't believe it."

"He's only been charged, not convicted," said the dour princess in front of me, swinging dark locks as she turned to face us. "And it's date rape, not the real kind."

"You're crazy," said the other kid. "It's multiple rape. There were several complainants."

"When was this?" I said.

"Last week. I don't know," said the boy.

"I saw him last week. That's when he borrowed my notes."

"Lucky you," said the boy, dead serious. "Just think what could have happened."

"Yes, just think," said the princess, mockingly. She knew. She saw through me. She saw right into my head, where I was too busy quivering with humiliation to bother with relief: All those girls—why not me?

"It's probably nothing anyway, just some girls trying to get attention," she said.

"That's classic," said the boy. "Have you never heard of the feminist movement?"

"Get some balls," said the girl. "Women lie."

The weedy-looking kid stared down at his notes. Part of my brain said, He is blinking away tears, but it seemed unkind even to think it. One of his fingers plucked at an absolutely wretched sweater that looked like it had been dragged down an alley and left in the rain, putty-coloured with grey flecks, too wide in the shoulders and bagging hopelessly over his bony wrists.

On a fresh piece of paper, I wrote, "Don't worry, she's just a bitch," folded it into neat squares and handed it across the aisle to him. The class was filling up. I could see the man with the hair hat at the very front of the hall, just beneath the lectern, just like usual.

The boy passed the paper back to me. "I'm not worried," it read. "But thanks."

"Passing notes," said the princess, who had twitched her hair around in time to catch this last transaction. "What a big boy you are."

"Fuck off," I said; he said nothing, just glanced at the piece of paper in my hand like it was diseased.

"All right, class, let's get this show on the road. We've got a lot of material to review today," said the prof, jean-clad and very blue-eyed. Smiling dismissively at us, the princess turned her attention toward him. He was the sort of professor who always had, gathered about him at the end of a lecture, a clamour of young women breathy with follow-up questions. The weedy-looking boy folded like an accordion over his yellow notepad, sucked on the end of his pen.

"Do you think I could borrow your notes?" I said to him after class. Despite my having practised this sentence for the previous fifty minutes, it came out altogether wrong, afflicted by a general phlegminess, and worse, I actually said, "Do I think you could borrow your notes?"

"Pardon?"

"Your notes. Could I borrow them, maybe? That guy has mine."

"You mean the rapist."

"Um, I guess."

"I don't know," said the boy, squinching into a black plastic jacket that bunched around the middle.

"We could go over them together. Get together sometime and go over them."

"Oh," he said. "I don't really need help studying."

"She's asking you out, little dork," said the princess, cinching the belt on a forest green coat before marching toward the professor, whose eyes glowed and glittered as he addressed, with charming intimacy, a tiny blond before the chalkboard.

"I'm not, really," I said, suddenly hot and damp, feverish almost. "Excuse me."

Smoke billowed by the doors as I exited the hall. The hair hat man stood there among a small group of fellow smokers. His hair was shaped like a hat. It was. I looked again, through wet eyes, and said, So there. You see. It is. The stone steps were slippery as I scurried down them.

"It's a personal safety device," he was saying, tapping a pocket. "There are evil people even among us."

"What's the cost?" said someone. It was the weedy-looking kid, framed in the doorway, neither in nor out.

I scurried and scurried over wet slabs until one nipped up and bit me. There was the skidding of a foot—mine—the lurch, the gasp, the fall, the crash, the hoarse expletive. Arse over teakettle, I imagined writing in my diary; and, the horror, the horror. Elbow banged and bookbag swatted the ground. Inside the bag, a glass bottle of iced tea shattered. Prone, I opened the top of the bag and had a look inside. It was ruin; ruin on a small scale, but ruin nevertheless.

Placing his cigarette almost formally upon the ashtray, the hair hat man came toward me. He was ripe with dignity. I could see it coming off him in waves. His hand curved under my arm as he lifted me up.

"Tell me," I said. "Tell me—would your personal safety device protect me from a situation such as this?"

"This is nothing," he said. "Years from now, you will laugh."

"So that's a no."

"Your bag, my dear."

"Thanks." It tinkled as he passed it to me. Everyone else had turned away, dispersing. They were lousy with previous commitments: telephones ringing, email unwritten, notes unstudied, friends guffawing, teachers flirting, beer to drink, girls to rape, lies to tell. They could not care less about my clumsiness, my efforts and attempts, my foolish, foolhardy falls.

His hat had brushed my cheek as he bent to pull me upright. It smelled of some ancient room, mint and cinnamon, just opened and released into modern-day air. It knew of nothing new and awful, only of the old and otherworldly, spices and dusty roads and deep shadows thrown at dusk. The shadows of two figures on horseback, one in a hat, looking for something, searching and seeking, and hopeful.

I would carry this home, too, but I would not share it. I did not know how.

What strange romance, I would write in my diary. What places impossible to travel.

COMFORT

WE ALL NEEDED COMFORT.

My niece woke up crying just before dawn, and for a moment, I was disoriented and thought there was a baby in the house. I put my palms to my breasts, expecting the milk to let down. Marvin did not move beside me. That can't be, I thought, as one hand met with the flat land of my left chest, arresting me into the present.

I lost the left one after the third baby had been weaned, when they told me surgery was the only alternative. Alternative to what? I meant to ask but did not. Alternative to death was the answer, of course, but perhaps doctors do not say such words out loud. This is what I said instead: "Thank God I got to nurse my babies." The man in white looked politely aside, but the nurse in the room smiled right through me. "That's right," she said. "Count your blessings."

I threw off the sheet and heaved out of our swampy bed. The mattress was like a sinkhole, but we could not afford to replace it on Marvin's teaching salary, or so he said. He gave me an allowance each week with which to buy groceries, handing me the envelope of thirty dollars in ten-dollar bills and saying, "This is bleeding us dry."

"What," I'd say. "What—eating is bleeding us dry?"

On the budget, I was able to purchase flour, sugar, salt, vinegar, oil, milk: items we could not bake or can or cook or grow or kill on our own. Our girls loved the Little House on the Prairie series of books, the constant labour, the calico dresses, the simple rewards of popcorn in the evenings or one clean sack of white sugar for special company cakes.

The child was snuffling, not crying, when I got to the bedroom door. "Girls," I said, "who was screaming?"

"Francie had a bad dream," said Katie, who was sharing the double bed. My eyes adjusted to the pale darkness, and I could see Katie hovering over Francie like a hen over an escaped chick.

Mary woke up too and called out from the cot in the corner, "Mommy? What's happening?"

"Hush," I said. "Go back to sleep, girls. Francie, come with me."

Her shoulders were bony, rigid, the body small and unprotected.

"Can I call my mom?" she said. Her eyes dilated wildly under the naked bathroom light, huge in the tiny pale face. She shivered in a long, thin T-shirt that said "Florida's Sunny Valley Express," the words encircling a picture of a glass of orange juice. Lord only knows where her mother had picked that up. My sister had not married well. She'd married for romance, or some semblance of it, and the words that came to mind when I saw that pair together were: You've dug your grave, now lie in it. But the child had no choice, and for her, my heart ached.

"Let's not bother your mother over this." I shook out the thermometer and popped it under her tongue. "I'll get you a glass of water while we wait."

When I returned, the child was straining to see herself in the mirror. I do not tolerate vanity in my own daughters, but there was something pathetic about the look trapped on the child's face when she'd thought she was all alone: admiration, a fixity in her eyes and lips that betrayed pleasure. If she had been one of my girls, I would have said,

"Pretty is as pretty does"; instead, I took the thermometer from her mouth. "Perfectly normal. You're not sick."

I waited in the hallway while she peed, leaning my head against the cool plaster wall. I was tired. I was the sort of tired that eats into your bones. You can feel it leaching into your skull; you are simultaneously chilled and hot. The toilet flushed. I heard the water running as she washed her hands. That showed something: good manners, good training. My sister tried her best.

She had briefed me over the phone to expect nightmares. "Francie hasn't been the same since her little friend drowned. I shudder every time I think of it."

"Don't let your imagination run away with you," I said. "That won't help."

"It will be good for Francie to be around your girls," said my sister. "She's been so lonely, and moping."

"We don't allow for moping around here," I said. You would think I was the elder sister, but I am not. I am two years younger, though taller and rounder. There was a time when the tables were turned. I remember my sister yanking me by the arm at a high-school dance: "What do you think you're doing? You're acting like a slut."

"Fuck off," I said. "Fuck off and go fuck yourself."

"What's up with your sister," my friend Leigh-Ann said, slurping from her can of Coke Plus. We called it Coke Plus because it was half vodka. You poured out the Coke and poured in the vodka. Leigh-Ann and I were dressed in the same style: bell bottoms that rode low under the belly button, cut-off T-shirts, feathered hair, blue eyeshadow. My T-shirt was pink, and across the breasts there was a yin-yang sign.

"What does that mean?" said Eddie Topinksy, brushing the sign with the back of his hand.

Leigh-Ann was two months pregnant, but she did not know it yet. After she found out, we both changed. We could hardly be the same. What did it feel like to have a baby? I wanted to know but could not ask. What did it feel like to have something inside you, kicking and punching? What did it feel like when it came out?

Leigh-Ann came home, and she said she had to wear pads in her bra to stop the milk from leaking everywhere. She made it sound like a joke: milk squirting across the room and hitting someone in the eye, milk like a water gun. The baby was gone to a better home. She never once said "the baby." Neither did I.

By then, I was wearing less makeup, only black mascara. By then, I was favouring baggy blouses that disguised my shape, long skirts in unflattering, dark colours, flat shoes or clogs. Leigh-Ann looked the same, laughed the same. She wanted to go out behind the school and smoke and drink Coke Plus. It wasn't even lunchtime. "We should really go to class," I said.

"When did you get so lame," she said.

I did not say anything. I was looking inside and seeing all the black areas excised, bit by bit, to be replaced by shining white surfaces that reflected everything and said nothing. Goodness and light, I whispered. Goodness and light.

There is a balance in families. My sister took up where I left off. That is how I saw it, and so, I also saw, I was to blame.

"Back to bed," I said to Francie. She held the glass of water in both hands, but I reached out and took it from her. "You'll go right to sleep." My hand shook on the water glass.

Marvin's alarm would be going off soon, not for his sake but for mine, and the new day would be under way already. I pulled the sheet over the child's small frame, her face tucked into the pillow. I smoothed the hair out of her eyes and kissed her on the forehead. She closed her eyes as if she were wishing something. Her lips moved involuntarily.

"Sleep tight," I said.

When I crawled in beside Marvin, he turned over so his back was to me. The mattress shifted like salt water and I was rolled into the middle, against him. “Can’t you stay on your own side?” he said.

“I didn’t know you were awake.”

“I’m not.”

The frilly white nightgown billowed and gathered uncomfortably around my thighs. Even in the heat of summer, we slept chastely, clothed. I shifted to pull the nightgown lower and the mattress bobbled like a ship at sea.

“Must you throw your weight around?” said Marvin.

“I’m sorry,” I said. It was cool in the early morning, and I was glad for his back against me. I was glad for the angry heat sliding off him in waves. The sheet over us was starched hard and smelled of fresh air. I breathed in deeply and was able to sleep.

~

When the alarm went, I pulled on my red bathrobe, so worn the terry cloth was matted like a mangy dog’s coat, and plugged in the noisy percolator. Marvin did not drink coffee; it was my one vice, I liked to say—two cups in the morning, doused with yellow cream and three heaping spoonfuls of sugar.

This was my ritual, waiting for the percolator, hands resting on the countertop at the window overlooking our small orchard and, beyond, the red barn. The kitchen was clean and still and untouched for the day.

I poured the coffee into a beautiful cup, delicate blue china etched with a pagoda beside a lake and thin stalk-like trees that might be bamboo.

I had only one like it, a gift from one of my mother's childless aunts, given for Christmas with a matching saucer. High school had come to a close, and I had turned inward. I considered attending Bible college. My parents were perplexed. "What do you care about the Bible?" God was not mentioned around our house, not even once. To say "God is calling me" was like passing gas at the dinner table.

My mother's aunt had been a benevolent adventuress, of sorts. She had visited China, delivering to orphaned children thousands of hand-knit booties and caps made by Women's Leagues all across Canada. She had been to India, too, and Egypt. Her apartment was crammed with trinkets from these journeys: framed maps on the walls, shelves of jade Buddhas and plastic flowers and strangely shaped vessels. She did not offer a Christmas gift to anyone else.

"I thought you'd like this," she said as explanation.

"I love it. I adore it." I floated to her on a cloud of sanctity and kissed her whiskery cheek. The world was wide open, and I could be anything. A gift like this seemed natural and deserved. I was marooned in my parents' house, sleeping in my childhood bed, working split shifts at a coffee shop, but this was temporary. My real life would start any minute—a life of service, of good, of offerings to the poor and needy. The cup was a portent from my real life.

I recalled all of this now without cynicism. I was grateful for the optimism of youth, its cosmetic power, its blind enthusiasms.

I carried the cup to the garden, a rectangular truck patch running the length of the house and beyond. It was too early for the whine of bugs. My feet were bare in the damp grasses. I could sit in the striped lawn chair, cool morning air moving around my ankles, until the coffee grew clammy in the cup and the cream turned to a skin.

"I am glad you like it," my mother's aunt said in response to my effusions. Her arms did not move from her sides, her posture composed and reserved. I thought her darling and eccentric. You may think that because I was wrapped in the flesh of holiness, I must have been solemn, even dour, but this was not so: I was as rash as ever, impulsive, quick to embrace and thoughtlessly discard.

"I will treasure it always," I said. My sister did not hear me. She was on the front porch smoking a cigarette by herself. Nobody minded. She had a weary presence that darkened a warm room, a thin presence like a knife blade or the smoke from a blown-out candle. My parents had thrown up their hands. They were waiting to see what colossal mistake she would make, although she had made none yet, that we knew of.

The screen door squeaked. Francie's head peeked out, T-shirt flapping at her knees, watching me like a rabbit watches a hawk. "Aunt Lucy?" she said. "Can I call my mom now, do you think?"

"Come here, honey." I placed the cup on the grass beside me. "The dog's tied up."

She stood nearby in bare feet but did not want to be touched. Neither of us mentioned her mother again. I pointed to the different vegetables, and she looked vaguely into some middle ground I could not see. A faint hum came from the bushes. The bugs were out and preparing for a day's battle. It was time to go inside.

The child spotted the cup as I bent to pick it up, and she wanted a closer look. I let her hold it. "It's the only one like it," I said. "It's unique."

"I'm careful," she said.

"Of course you are."

She carried the cup to the house for me, and in the kitchen, she placed it in my hands ceremoniously. There were blades of grass stuck to her feet, and to mine. The kitchen was already warm. I reached to open the windows over the sink, and when I turned, she was gone. Water was running upstairs. It was time to set the table for breakfast, to break eggs into a silver bowl, to slice homemade oatmeal bread for toast.

Marvin was the last to make it to the kitchen. I waited until he'd arrived to serve the eggs and sausage. I was sweating under the bathrobe but did not want to take it off. Marvin disliked the sight of the one breast hanging loose under the thin white gown, although one breast seemed to me less obscene, somehow, androgynous, like a stumpy arm.

~

We met the summer I turned twenty-two. I spent four years after high school living in my parents' house, sleeping in my childhood bed, working up to manager at the coffee shop. My savings account was substantial, my optimism diminished.

I attended the Holy Bible Church in a strip mall, where we sang hymns accompanied by electric guitars and bongo drums. The front of the sanctuary was a mess of electrical cords and amps, like a high-school gym on the night of a dance. Services were held Sunday mornings and Wednesday evenings. I met Marvin at the bus stop by the strip mall after a Wednesday evening service. He was the one who said, “Hello, how are you?” I was just being polite. He had never heard of the Holy Bible Church. He had never read the Bible. He preferred *Harrowsmith* magazine. He would build a house with his own hands someday.

“Out of straw bales,” he said. We climbed onto the bus together and chose to share a seat at the back.

“I don’t understand,” I said. “Wouldn’t it be a fire hazard?”

“It’s a new technique. Someday, all of these buildings will be straw-bale buildings.” His favourite word was “someday,” although I did not guess that yet. His someday was filled with the promise of hardship and labour, sacrifice and routine.

The land we bought, with a down payment from my bank account, was an eerie flat stretch in the midst of rolling fields near Paris, Ontario. It had a house on it, shingled in grey with a sloping roof. The upstairs was like a furnace in summer. Marvin was seduced by the dilapidated swarm of yellow cherry trees between house and barn. He wanted a riding lawn mower. He wanted a red tractor. He wanted a pickup truck, any colour, with pulling capacity and a dusty flatbed.

"What about the straw bales?" I whispered, pregnant with Steph, our first, and trying not to vomit in front of the real estate agent.

"Oh, someday," Marvin said. "Not now."

Our wedding at the Holy Bible Church had been raucous, although neither of us was. Someone passed out tambourines. My parents sat on folding chairs in the front row, watching their hands and blushing for us. This is our successful daughter? I could hear them thinking. This is the best we've got? My sister was in Montreal and did not have the bus fare to make it home for the wedding. A lie. She did not know there was a wedding. We had not spoken for nearly a year.

"That was a crazy wedding," said Marvin afterward. "Those people are crazy."

"You don't have to come to church just because I go," I said.

"You're not going any more," he said.

The special thing about this fight was the location: in the honeymoon suite at a Holiday Inn. The fabric on the bedspread was rough, like curtains, and I knelt in the middle of the vast mattress in panties and a bra.

"What do you mean, I'm not going?"

"You promised to obey."

"That wasn't literal."

"Put on some clothes. I can't talk to you like that."

The special thing about this fight was his disgust, newly born and fully developed, ripening from the curl in his lip. He could not look at me. I spread my legs and sat on my bottom, spread my legs wide and leaned back on my elbows, taunting him.

"What?" I said. I stroked the inside of one thigh with a finger.

He pulled the bedspread like a giant pastry shell and wrapped me up, even my face. "Cover yourself now," he said. "Be decent."

In my heart, I could not confess that I had made a mistake. The struggle I made against him was purely for form, and because I could not breathe properly. "Okay," I said. "Okay. I won't go any more."

Marvin gently drew the blanket from my face. He kissed my temples, my cheekbones, my lips. "You are as pretty as a pink flower," he said. Lack of oxygen, my mind replied, but I was moved nevertheless. "Let's never fight again," he said. Against my lower belly and through the bunched bedspread, I could feel his erection. I let my head fall back, exposing my neck like the stem of a flower snapped.

"Don't be so stingy with the sausage," said Marvin, holding his knife and fork expectantly, one in each hand. He reminded me of a child. I reached through the spitting grease and plucked another link from the pan. He would hate my fingers touching the meat directly, but he would not know how to express it delicately.

I poured my second cup of coffee and stood in front of the kitchen sink, hip dug into the counter.

"That coffee's going to kill you one of these days," said Marvin, eyeing me. He was calculating whether he should request more sausage or stand and get it for himself.

"Have another piece of sausage," I said. "There's plenty." I did not move to assist him.

"What about me?" said Katie. "I want more too."

I turned to the window and watched the cherries bobbing in the breeze, heavy and full, some plopping to the ground, where the squirrels and birds would fight for them and they would rot into the earth. The scene at the table stayed in my mind like a little tableau that held no meaning, as if I'd come upon them all in a dream or was passing a painting at a museum, my head turned for this moment to contemplate a mystery that had no connection to me.

"Lucy?" said Marvin. "The sausage?"

"Mom?" said Katie. "Can I, can I?"

I set the cup in the middle of the clean, white counter and walked to the stove. "Today, you're going to pick the cherries, girls," I said.

~

When my sister gave birth to a daughter, we rejoiced. By "we," I mean my sister and I. She phoned from the hospital. Her baby was sleeping in a bassinet beside the bed. I imagined white blankets, white pillows, white sheets, a white gown, the baby swaddled in white with a white cap covering its pale head.

"I never knew," said my sister. "I never knew this joy."

"Of course not," I said. "There is nothing like it."

Her husband was not there. He was off celebrating.

"Where's Gianni?" I could not help asking.

"Oh, you know. Out with the guys." Nothing could cut through her pleasure, nothing could dim the sunlight sliding through the hospital window, anointing her baby girl.

This was little Francie; this was her day. Sisters had no choice but to bear each other up when the moment arrived. We did not forget anything, but we could go on when the occasion called for it. I would not mention Gianni again during the entire conversation. I would bite my tongue.

"Where are Mom and Dad?"

"They're on their way. 'Nothing but daughters and granddaughters,' they said."

"But they aren't complaining, surely?"

"Who can know."

We rejoiced despite Gianni. We rejoiced while my two-year-old wandered off and discovered the kitchen compost bin; the phone cord did not reach that far. We stopped rejoicing when Marvin came in for lunch and discovered coffee grounds all over the linoleum.

My sister was a small woman and her baby a small baby, pallid, grey, splashed with a fiery rash. When they visited the farm, I held the infant, and Gianni pressed kisses into the nape of my sister's neck. He could not understand why there was no beer in the house. He ran his hands over my sister's soft belly and up under her breasts. "This is an amazing woman," he said. "Look at this baby. Just look at her."

"I hate that guy," said Marvin. "If any of my daughters marries a guy like that, I'll kill her myself."

~

I dashed upstairs to change. It wasn't a dash so much as a haul. I was breathless by the time I reached the top step, one hand on the carved walnut railing, the other clasping the lapels of my bathrobe, holding them together against my throat. I rested in front of the small window at the top of the stairs, looking out over a field of corn. This is nothing: I mouthed the words. This is nothing.

In the bedroom, I shed everything and stood in the middle of the floor, catching my reflection in the wavy mirror over the bureau. A warped figure, thighs and breast in the wrong proportions, as if some mysterious geometry were working against me. I never got closer to the mirror than this. I never looked directly.

After all this time, it ought not to have mattered so much. Change besets us, every one.

Fresh underwear, a fresh blue dress with cornflowers. I ran cool water over a comb in the narrow bathroom and pulled it through my hair, splashed my face, rinsed my mouth. The skin at my wrist was already healing into a dark slash.

Yesterday, the dog had been running loose. "Get that fucker away from me," Gianni said with his window rolled up. Francie's white face stared from the back seat.

Marvin yanked the dog off by its collar. "This old bitch is harmless." He was cock-eyed with happiness, watching Gianni sweat.

"Oh, for Christ's sake." My sister hauled herself from the car, threw open the trunk for Francie's suitcase.

"You shouldn't carry that," said Gianni. His moustache drooped. My sister was nine months pregnant, huffing and puffing like a beached walrus.

"Allow me," said Marvin, playing the gentleman. Released, the dog leapt madly at Gianni's window, tracking saliva. The child was near tears.

"Marvin," I said. He was carrying Francie's suitcase to the porch. "Marvin, get that dog out of here." I made a grab for its collar. Yellow teeth grazed my wrist, drawing blood; it was an act so straightforward and simple, not even punctuated by a growl, that it seemed mechanical. For Francie's sake, I turned my wrist to hide the bleeding.

"Marvin," I said again, my hand shaking against the folds of my dress.

He had not seen. Irritation hardened his shoulders as he dragged the dog to the barn and locked it in.

Gianni stepped from the car and examined the door for scratches. "I just had this thing repainted," he said. My sister held Francie's head against her belly. "I'm going to miss you, my baby. I'm going to miss you. Be good." That was all. They would be on their way.

I wrapped my arms around the child as the car drove down the lane. "We're going to have a lovely holiday together," I said. Francie broke free. She had seen the blood on my wrist. Her strange dark eyes stared through me to a blotch in the sky, a scab of light I could not see.

The girls picked two baskets of cherries each. I pitted the fruit into the sink and lined up scalded Mason jars on the counter. Syrup bubbled on the stove. A halo of heat rose and sat half an inch over the circumference of my skin. I could feel every breath pushing up my ribcage, collapsing it. There was a hum to the house, and to the yard.

The knock on the door was so quiet that I did not register it.

"Hello?" called a voice. "Ma'am? Anyone at home?"

A strange car was parked in the lane, under the black walnut tree. My hands were pinched and red from the work, and I wiped them on my skirt.

"What do you want," I said, opening the screen door a fraction. My head pounded with blood, not from anger, from dizziness. The sun was too bright.

"Oh my good God," said the man, who wore a hat and a suit, inappropriately heavy for a day like today. "You're Leigh-Ann's friend. I can't remember your name. Leigh-Ann's friend from high school." Colour rose in his face, up to the brim of the hat, which I saw now was not a hat. It was made of hair and grew directly from his scalp. The scene was at a remove from me, the punchline to a joke I could not recall, the inner lining of a dream.

"Excuse me?" I said, as if floating through clear water, blurred and weightless.

"Leigh-Ann. You were best friends for a few years. Before . . ." He did not continue.

"I remember Leigh-Ann." The scene resolved like a camera lens clicking into focus. My phantom breast ached as I clutched the screen door, a thin ring of rage spinning under my ribs. His presence, his hair hat, were uncalled for, an accident, a misfortune, a blemish on an otherwise clean, calculated day that should have held nothing but the ordinary reminders and warnings. No right, I thought. He has no right.

"I'm her father."

"Of course."

He set down the briefcase he'd been carrying and looked into my face. "You would be thirty-five now?"

"Thirty-six."

There were tears in his eyes and he did not speak, patting in his coat pockets for a Kleenex.

"What do you want," I said again. "Whatever you're selling, I doubt we'll take it. We are on a tight budget."

"It doesn't matter now," he said, pushing aside the briefcase with his foot, as if to make it invisible. "This seems like a miracle."

"I haven't seen Leigh-Ann for years," I said.

"No," he said. "Nor has anyone."

"Right," I said.

"You were such good friends. Like twins."

"People go their different ways. People change. They move on."

"Her mother and I thought often of you in the years afterward."

I looked down my dress to my feet, in rubber flip-flops. I had discarded Leigh-Ann like everything else I had rid myself of: cleanly, without regret, brutally. Nothing in me wanted to know more about her fate. Her fate held the secret of what might have become of me; worse, of what had become of me, a person who would turn away at any cost.

"You have a family?" said the man. A trickle of sweat crept down his brow and he winked it away. "This lovely farm."

"I'm sorry," I said. "I'm sorry I cannot help you. We don't want whatever you are selling."

"You have had a lucky life," he said.

"Please," I said. "Please leave now."

"She is missing, you know. She has been missing for ten years."

"Get out of here."

I could see Marvin climbing off the tractor, walking to the dog, unsnapping its chain.

My arms brushed the air with giant sweeps. "Go away, now."

The dog tore across the stones, brindled head bobbing heavily. The man danced to the car, briefcase flapping. I turned away, my fingers slipping from the screen door, metallic with sweat. The kitchen was filled with steam, and I snapped off the burner under the syrup. Three jars were packed with yellow cherries, and my hands moved automatically, squeezing out more pits, filling the jars. By the time the steam had cleared from the windows, the car had vanished, and so had the man.

The dog was loose again. Poor Francie.

The phone rang. It was the message I had been expecting: a new sister for Francie, a new daughter for my sister. We did not speak long, Gianni and I. "Very good," I said, but my throat could not form the proper platitudes. Water was boiling. I needed to place the packed jars into the canner.

I was cutting up cooked potatoes for a salad when Francie and Mary arrived at the house, safely, despite the dog careening free through the fields. Mary was very pink in the cheeks, and Francie would not look at either of us.

"Here you are. I have good news," I said, but something in me had hardened, some bare chunk of flesh had calcified, and I could feel neither pity nor joy. "You have a new sister," I told Francie. I handed her a sugar cookie, and one for Mary, too. We turned away from each other. Whatever the child was thinking, I could not decipher, and did not attempt it.

Forget comfort: when the moment arrives, it will be the opposite we stumble against.

When Mary came calling into the kitchen a while later, I looked into her face and saw her lips moving but did not hear anything.

"Go and play," I said. "Lunch will be ready soon."

QUEENIE, MY HEART

THERE WAS A SONG in my head I could not place. Behind the counter, I hummed it softly, the same line over and over. Nobody noticed. If they noticed anything, it was my size. I did not mind. You got used to almost anything, and this was something I'd had around me for a while: corpulence, excess, a comforting girth wrapped now in a brown-and-orange smock.

On afternoons like this one, blinds were drawn over the line of west-facing windows and a skin of heat sulphured the air.

"May I take your order?" I said, a thousand times a day. The name "Queenie" was embroidered above my left breast, but no one called me that, not even Tiem, flitting like a flea behind me. She called me "Hey there," sometimes "Honey." Her dark, pimpled skin was a mask of calculated indifference.

"Large double double," said the man whose hair was shaped into a hat. I could not tell you what sort of hat. With hair, it was difficult to say.

"Will that be all?" I said.

I had never seen him here before. He was an old man, tall, shoulders stooped but defiant. Ha ha! his posture seemed to say.

"That will be a dollar twenty-three," I said. The man spent some time digging through an inner coat pocket, until people waiting in line were coughing and shuffling their feet.

"A dollar twenty-three," I said again. I did not raise my voice. I was still humming.

The man met my eyes. His were rough, deep in the crinkled and worn skin. His hand came slowly out from the inner reaches of his coat. I was afraid, and then, as Tiem squished past my rump to get to the pastry counter, not afraid. Fear came and went like that, knocked away by another distraction.

Exact change. Our hands met, his ropy and palsied, mine sweating, professional.

"Next, please," I said.

~

Sometimes girls from the Catholic high school said unpleasant things. Mostly, they were as polite as you might expect teenage girls to be, their skirts rolled up at the waist, eyes rimmed in black, skin lined and hard. They came here to smoke. It was the heavy-set girl, legs blotching pink and white between sock and skirt, who said the most unpleasant things. In my mind, I told her, It's not so bad. It's not so bad, really, being like this. To her face, I was closed, bored, an elephant squatting under leafy trees waiting for the men with guns to pass.

I wasn't always like this: this shape. It crept up on me; it ballooned and blossomed. I could no longer say that I was sorry for any of it. Wasn't that strange.

Today, during a lull, Tiem sat at a table and was quiet. "Have you seen that guy before, the one with the hair hat?" I said.

"Hair hat?" said Tiem, sucking on a cigarette.

"His hair was shaped into a hat," I said.

"What did he order?" said Tiem. Her face twitched and ash spilled everywhere as she jabbed at an abandoned coffee cup.

"Nothing special."

"No," said Tiem. "Never seen him."

I moved to clean more tables. The cloth in my hand was grey and stank of rotting fibres. People will leave anything behind on a coffee shop table, because anything becomes anonymous here. I scooped, I wiped down, I gathered ash, matches, a paper napkin stained with lipstick into my palm to throw out. All the time, I wondered about the hat. Maybe it wasn't his hair. Maybe it was just an awful hat.

Without effort, I incorporated him into an ongoing fantasy. I am working the night shift, and he returns. The radio plays a sugary song as our hands touch accidentally across the counter. Coffee splashes and spills. Oh dear, now look what I've done! I say. And he says, May I help you with that? Please, allow me. He slips behind the counter too. We fall to our knees, me with a damp cloth to swab up the mess, but he puts out his hand to stop me. Excuse me, let me, here, there: he says all of these things, and more, all in a confusion. With barely enough room for me to squeeze to the floor, we are prone, beautifully. Ahh. Strokes and motions of the mouth, hands on breasts, hands in hair. Hat hair. What will it feel like? Springy, textured, grizzled, firm.

I was disturbed by the door opening, and cold winter air, standing near the windows with the smelly cloth clutched between my fingers. Tiem had disappeared, to the bathrooms or to call her troublesome boyfriend. I eased behind the counter to the grim-faced customer.

"Haven't got all day," he muttered.

"May I take your order?"

I was humming the song again, and the words came to me of a sudden: *Sometimes I feel like a motherless child*. The day progressed as you might expect. The sun expired and the room went from too hot to too cool. Tiem opened the blinds. My shift was over.

"Don't forget your tips," said Tiem. She had on her coat with the fake fur collar and was bent over the counter, where coins were divided into two equal piles.

"Thanks," I said. The dimes made a clatter in my pockets, their weight like something wasted. I was outside now. I was thrown into the street, carrying in my head the light of the coffee shop, the smell of icing sugar on donuts and waterlogged coffee grounds. Out here was darkness, a rush of traffic and lights. People went out of their way to avoid brushing against one another.

The back-alley entrance was lit by a single square floodlight that sent a sickening glare over concrete walls. One of the walls had a sheltered ledge built into it, usually occupied. The girl in the pink plastic jacket sat beside the man who claimed this spot.

"Good night," said the man, tipping an imaginary hat. He was always polite. The girl's face carried the familiar round stamp of Down's syndrome.

"Good night," I said, averting my eyes, grocery bags biting into swollen palms.

"Pa, I'm home!" I called before puffing up the long straight staircase. Here, my mind was calmed and emptied, all fears called back by the rattle of the key in the door, the warmth of this place, its worn linoleum floors freckled in turquoise and gold, its dust-ridden air and persistent odour of roasted garlic rising from the Caribbean restaurant below.

Pa must have been resting.

Ah, Queenie, there you are, he would greet me, shuffling to the kitchen in his matted blue slippers to put the kettle on. Sit down and I will make us a cup of soup. Would you like mushroom or chicken noodle?

I'll put the kettle on, I thought. Packets of soup littered the kitchen counter, cubes of bouillon, instant noodles, flavoured oatmeal. Pa didn't cook; he reconstituted. I saw myself moving around the room, lifting the kettle, turning off the tap. I was still wearing my coat, too tired to remove it, too perfectly warm.

Heating grates flared to life, rats squirrelled in the walls, the kettle rocked on the burner. In the midst of this bustle, a heaviness came over me, inevitable, dull.

I knew.

There was nothingness here, a stillness that would not be disturbed. The apartment had been turned inside out and emptied.

"Pa?" My voice was locked in my throat.

Everything slipped through and exited my mind but this: the stairs, the grey pocked walls, a strangeness entering the air and pitching these stairs, these walls, into chaos. The molecules in the plaster were in motion. Nothing was solid. My body floated up the steps, weightless and supreme. There was the cactus on the ledge halfway up, and the potted spider fern. My chest ached. I knew my hand was on my heart, but I could not feel either.

"Pa?"

A stream of light slid from under the bathroom door. I knocked.

"Pa?"

The poster of Audrey Hepburn with cigarette in holder and bright black bangs hung as usual beside the door frame. The handle jostled open without resistance.

"Pa," I said, thinking, Thank God the water wasn't left running.

Heart failure, perhaps. Blue and bent, he floated under the surface of the water, shrunken penis lapping against thigh. The water was cool on my hand. I reached between his knotted ankles and pulled the plug.

~

When my mother left home, she was led to the back seat of a purple, plushy sedan and driven to a long-term care facility, and not the good sort—the sort where they confiscate your pension cheque, such as it may be, as payment. Pa and I stood aside and hoped for the best. Where am I going? she asked the driver, who did not return my pressed-on smile. Not back to that stinking trailer!

My father left home in an ambulance, already dead.

The kettle boiled dry on the stove and began to melt and twist in on itself. It made a funny stink in the air, which someone commented on, the one with the moustache. The two of us were standing in the hallway, waiting for something; I was not sure what. “Dammit,” I said, and rushed to the kitchen. I scorched a perfectly good dish-cloth pitching the remains into the kitchen sink while the ambulance men were upstairs, strapping my father’s body to a stretcher.

“I should have bought the whistling kind,” I said.

“Pardon?” said the one with the moustache. He seemed to be in charge. He had followed me to the kitchen doorway.

“Excuse me,” I said. I ran cold water and waited as the steam pulsed up and around me in a great wave.

I was still standing at the sink after the ambulance left. There was paperwork to be filled out. I had not been listening while the man with the moustache explained, and I became frightened, imagining my father’s body trapped and lost in the underbelly of a brown brick institution. My face was wet, but it seemed to be from the steam, not from anything like tears. When I brushed the skin with the palm of my hand, it was cold.

Nobody was left. I was dizzy, as if nothing was holding me up, or nobody. You can think about death, and understand it, and still turn at the creak of a floorboard, expecting the face that is gone. What nobody tells you about absence is how near the dead will seem: just around the corner, in the next room.

I saw my pa like a horse sees a shiver of wind and shies aside. The horse keeps its head turned toward the thing it cannot see.

Ma, I thought. Ma, nesting among vile green afghans in a wheeled chair, singing, "Mares eat oats and does eat oats and little lambs eat ivy. A kid'll eat ivy too, wouldn't you?"

What do you know about mares? I thought, the first time I heard her sing this song.

"Lordy, your mother does sing a pretty tune," said the woman tucking blankets around Ma, her hair hanging in strings around a sweating face. That was the first I'd heard of it. She did not sing when I was a child.

Pa visited Ma often.

"She was a good woman," he would say, looking at me slyly out of the corner of his eye, waiting for my reply, his tone hearty and defiant. I did not disagree. Go ahead, Pa. Say it over and over, and we'll all feel the better for it.

The thought of going there alone, puffing up those yellow, broadloomed stairs to the third floor, wheezing in the smell of stale tuna casserole and ancient chicken soup, made me turn my head again. The doorway to the kitchen was empty.

When we had horses, our trailer sat on rocky ground outside a dumpy town, one main street with windows shuttered and blinkered and waiting for tourist season, when the money came in. Our land was worthless, swampy in low-lying areas and encrusted with flagrant mounds of the Canadian Shield; as a teenager, I could see this for myself and could tell Pa so. Pa never wavered.

He had seen something else from the beginning—a bargain—and he would believe he was a lucky man for as long as he lived. The barn was solid and wired. A few stakes in the ground and we had an electric fence for a corral. The co-op in town was hiring. The trailer came with the land.

"It's rusted and filthy and the foundation is cracking," said Ma.

"Welcome home," said Pa.

We would raise horses, board horses, breed horses, break horses.

I was ten. I loved horses. When the wind whipped over the rocks, flattening the brown grass and stinging my eyes, I felt a thrill, a quiver, as if I were a pioneer gazing across new lands, braving the elements, making a brand-new life out of nothing.

Pa sat on a bale of hay in the barn and pointed here and there while I munched on a snack. In the corner would be the tack room, with gleaming, soft leather. Smooth concrete flooring would cover this dirt, sturdy stall doors sliding open on oiled tracks and the horses within raising great, gentle heads, their coats glossy from a diet of oats, a regular grooming schedule, beds of clean straw.

Ma came to the barn door and squinted. "The day you make a dime off a horse is the day I win the Jesus-effing lottery," she said.

"If I listened to you, I'd be slitting my throat in the streets," said Pa. It was a horrible picture. I saw the blood running everywhere. "Why can't you be happy for me?" he said. "This is my dream come true."

"Ruined. We're ruined," said Ma.

Pa laughed.

"Put down that donut or I'll slap you across the head," said Ma, turning on me. I could feel sugar dusting my lips and chin like baby powder.

"Let her be. She's only a girl," said Pa.

On and on the argument would go. It would make its own wind and puff itself across the ocean of afternoon and evening. It would chase us out of the barn and all the way to the trailer. It would stand in the kitchenette and throw pots in the sink and drink shots of whisky.

I would go to my room. I had a shelf of books, and more books in cardboard boxes at the end of the bed. They smelled musty, like the damp basement libraries they'd come from. My grandma sent them to me, with the covers ripped off. She bought them at book sales and would print on the title page: "To My Queenie, with Love from Gran." The stories were mostly about girls and horses. The horses were wild, untrainable, broken-down. The girls were orphans or outcasts, dreamers who spotted valour in a mangy, worn-out beast. Together, they made each other into something different—brave, admired, free.

The first horse Pa bought was like the horses in the books: skittish, scared, young, and thin, ribs rasping against skin. His head was proud and fine. He bucked and kicked and bit. Pa got him for three hundred dollars from an old man up north who threw into the deal a second pony, a nasty little Shetland-type with a sweet forelock and an evil eye.

"She'll never be any use to anyone," said Pa. "But that other one's a champion. Look at his head, Queenie. He's got heart."

I named him Smoky for his grey speckled coat, which was almost black in some lights.

"He's yours to look after," said Pa, and my stomach filled up with happiness.

Then came the hard part: looking after him. My hands shook as I groomed his coat and his ears flattened to his skull, tail swatted the air. I cinched the girth strap around his bony ribs and rode him up and down the lane. We took a walking pace, Smoky sidling away from any rustle in the raspberry canes, head flung high.

"Don't take any crap from a horse," called Pa from the concrete slab in front of the trailer. He believed in the old-fashioned style of breaking a horse.

"That horse is going to kill her," said Ma. She was dressed for a shift at the Golden Dragon, the Chinese-Canadian restaurant downtown. Her hair was pulled into a sleek bun, and she wore lipstick and tightly belted black slacks.

"Mmm-mmm," said Pa, kissing Ma on the lips.

"Don't muss my hair."

Two months later, Smoky still skidded away from me, pinned his ears, quivered with fear. The hand I ran along his neck was timid. I never gave him a friendly slap under the mane like Pa did. "You've got to show him who's boss."

"Ready for a ride?" I said, and Smoky rolled his eyes. I jammed the bit between his teeth and draped the blue-and-white plastic reins over the saddle's horn. This was a late-spring weekend, when it was still cold outside. Up and down the lane we walked. I was not wearing mitts, and my hands were red and stiff on the braided reins.

"Easy boy," I said as the screen door slammed, splat.

"Don't you slam that door on me," said Ma. We could hear her halfway down the lane. There was the sound of something being smashed.

Pa rushed across the grass, punching the air with his arms. His mouth worked angrily, but nothing came out.

"Don't be scared," I said to Smoky. My hands shook wildly, thumbs knocking against his neck. "Don't be scared, don't be scared."

"Goddamn your mother," Pa said, steaming across the gravel toward us, but he wasn't looking at me or even at Smoky. His eyes were blind, the whirling arms, the swearing. Smoky backed away, hoofs scattering stones.

"Easy, easy," I said and tugged the reins, trying to turn him. It was the wrong thing to do. Smoky's head came back into my lap, and he reared up.

Pa was underneath us, grabbing the reins and yanking Smoky down. "Useless bloody animal," said Pa.

A strained noise came from Smoky's throat: fear. The metal bit tore into his mouth. I was buried in his mane, my arms wrapped around his damp thin neck, feeling soft hair against my lips. The sweet, dusty stink of horse flesh was everywhere. I breathed in horse, breathed in Smoky, then he slipped out from under me. I was rolling, falling, dragging myself across the lane on elbows. Smoky's hoofs danced like knives flashing.

"Pa," I said, thrashing through the raspberry canes. "Stop hitting him."

"Have you lost your mind?" said Ma from the concrete porch. She was still wearing her bathrobe and fresh from the shower. I could see her hair loose over her shoulders, wet.

Pa lost hold of the reins and stumbled. Smoky turned tail and kicked with both hind legs. There was a noise in the air, a wooden thump that sounded like bone being crushed. Pa's groans were grunts, air caught in the back of the throat. Ma ran toward us, barefoot, hair streaming behind her.

"Horace, Horace, Horace!" she cried. "Don't die on me, Horace!"

I caught Smoky far down the road in a muddy spring pasture. Our secret was that he kicked me too, out there in the field. But not so hard. The blow landed on my upper thigh, where the skin bloomed for weeks. Whenever I saw the yellows and purples, I thought of him, also of wildflowers crowding the ruts and ditches we walked in on our way home.

Pa had called the horse dealer. Smoky would have to leave.

"He was never going to amount to anything," he said, eating a handful of aspirin. He could barely stand from the pain. "Cut your losses, I say."

"If you'd listened to me in the first place," said Ma.

"How much longer till these kick in?" said Pa.

"I can't stand it," said Ma. "I'm taking you to town."

They were gone, to emergency, when the horse dealer rattled up the lane in a pickup with a cattle van hitched behind. I led Smoky up the ramp. His hoofs echoed. The van was too big for one skinny horse. I stood by Smoky's head while the man tied his halter to the side with baler twine. The velour of his muzzle was as soft as moss, softer. I thought, I am touching him for the last time.

"Don't be scared."

"He's not a bad sort," said the horse dealer. "Maybe he'll sell."

A lot of horses would never sell: too mean, too scared, too ugly, too broken. These went for meat. I knew about this instinctively; nobody had to say it out loud.

Smoky's eyes rolled white. The horse dealer lifted the metal ramp and slammed it shut. Smoky called out, a thin, whinnying cry. I stood still and alone in the gravel in front of the barn. There was the sound of Smoky's ragged hoofs against metal as the van pulled down the lane.

I cried until the skin around my eyes stung from the salt. I sat down hard on the gravel and cried, but this did not satisfy me, and I had to run, down the lane, into the wet spring dirt, the brown rotten weeds.

“Smoky, I love you,” I screamed at the mud, even as I knew that this was a silly display, that it answered nothing and meant nothing. Inside some other part of my head, I was as silent as a dumb, sick beast. I squatted on a chilly slab of rock and the sky passed over me, thick and colourless.

Back at the trailer, Pa was jovial from the painkillers.

“Don’t take it so hard, Queenie,” he said. “A horse is a horse. There will be other horses.”

“Over my dead body,” said Ma. She was doing a paint-by-numbers picture of Niagara Falls in oils. She had spread her art supplies on the plastic tablecloth. It soothed the nerves, she said. Everyone would have to get his own dinner tonight. There was leftover shepherd’s pie in the fridge.

“Queenie’s having no trouble eating,” Pa said.

He wanted everything normal and forgotten, I saw that.

“She’s a good little girl, our Queenie,” said Pa.

“Little,” snorted Ma, daubing glassy blue into the sky. She could say such things with a placidity that passed for kindness, and I was glad, temporarily, that I had this mother.

Years later, when I first heard Ma singing—“Oh flower of Scotland, when will we see your likes again?”—I felt this same gratitude. It was her way of pointing out the truth, after all; she had found a new way, through that muzzled brain. My gratitude restored me, for the moment, as it had before. I was able to walk to Pa and hold his hand as he wished. I was able to say, as then, "It's okay, Pa."

~

"It's okay," I said to the kitchen, the empty doorway. "I'll go and tell her."

I called the home first, to see whether such a late visit would be acceptable.

"I have sad news," I said to the girl who answered. "I would like to see my mother."

"Come over whenever," said the girl. "I'm here all night."

I decided to splurge and hail a cab. I imagined myself saying, "Mother, I have sad news." There was something soft about the words, something untrue. I imagined myself saying, "Pa is dead."

The man and the girl in the alley had been asleep. Their faces were patterned with lines, slippery and slack. The door must have woken them, sleeping on the edge. They sat up to watch me pass but lowered their eyes. The man held an imaginary hat against his heart; this is what I took it to be. Something was held against his heart, something imaginary. Even in winter, the alley stank of urine and the call of a siren rose from the street nearby. I was a ship at sea, rocking and bobbing in a pool of calm.

"Sorry about your dad," said the girl, giggling. She did not mean to giggle, that was clear. In all other ways, she was dignified, head cocked, eyes wet.

They knew all about the surface of my life, and his. They had seen Pa shuffle through this alley and out into open sunlight. He would have been wearing his dented hat. They had seen me take Pa by the arm and lead him elsewhere, or back here. They had seen him leave, finally.

I looked into the girl's face, smeared with dirt, her teeth glossy white. I could not remember ever looking at her directly, the way you avoid the face of the sun.

"Thank you," I said. I fished in my pocket, past the fountain of dimes, and wrapped my fingers around the twenty-dollar bill. I would take the subway instead. The least I could do.

Is there any mystery in fortune, really? Is there any mystery in luck? You can fall into and out of it like tripping over a pocket in the surface of the earth. I stood with my back against the tiled subway wall, and the train rushed down the track. I had let my hair out of the bun, and it straggled and swirled at my shoulders. The doors opened directly in front of me.

He was waiting to get off. I was the only one waiting to get on, at these doors. We were suspended on either side, like bugs in amber. When the glass parted, he squeezed himself flat so that I could pass by. The smell of him was powdery, genteel, a man who would scrupulously apply aftershave to a stinging chin. Nor was he as old this time; the ropes of his hands were strong. If they shook when they brushed the sleeve of my coat, it was for another reason, one I had not calculated before.

He did not get off. He chose a seat near mine, then stood and chose one even closer.

"Oh," I said. Just that, almost a sigh. He leaned in, his hair hat glancing my ear, as if he knew the word was meant for him, and so I breathed it again, "Oh."

My reflection in the window opposite was unreadable, even to me, a series of blurs and etches. It was a night for doing the least, and so I closed my eyes. The least I could do would carry me elsewhere, to some place I had failed to foresee. What was it, there on my tongue, a word that would not come. The lights flickered. The smell of him was green and dusty, the smell of a bale of hay in mid-winter. The word waited for me to release it.

Found.

HARASSMENT

CARLOS SAID, "What's a guy like that doing wandering the streets?"

And Linda said, "He wasn't wandering the streets. He was in a coffee shop. Weren't you paying attention?" This was in the kitchen at their place. Carlos was burning something on the stove for our suppers.

"Watch what you're doing, Carlos," I said. He was looking at me instead of the pot on the stove, kind of smiling.

"You're making it up, right?" he said. "Just to see what we'll say."

Like that was something I did every day. I'm not that interesting, to tell the truth. Would I make up a guy with his hair shaped like a hat?

"I think that stuff is burning or something," I said. "I think I smell smoke."

~

The next time I saw Carlos and Linda, we bumped into each other on the street outside their place. I was just off work and happened to be passing by.

"Are you hungry?" said Carlos, or something like that, something nice and polite.

"You bet I am," I said.

Linda was a beautiful girl, long dark hair and a face like a bowl of milk. Carlos was okay too, although you saw them together and thought, Now, what's she doing with him? He had the kind of beady eyes that made him look a little weaselly, like he might try to cheat you out of something. It wasn't true. He was very generous. He made macaroni and cheese that afternoon, just because I mentioned that I hadn't had time for a snack yet.

I worked in the mornings before it got too hot. I planted flowers and did the weeding and such for municipal sites, by which I mean parks. They call them municipal sites at the headquarters. I was in charge of two parks. I did the mowing and picking up the trash, and I got to drive the pickup truck, although I wasn't senior management or anything. Maybe someday.

There was a girl who worked with me at that time, very serious and shy.

"What's a pretty girl like you doing hanging out with a guy like me?" I said to her, just teasing, and she would go all quiet and wouldn't look at me. To tell the truth, she wasn't that pretty, but I didn't mind. I got her to do the easy stuff, like riding the mower, while I got dirty.

"Pretty girls like you aren't made for getting dirty," I told her, but she just put on a dark face like she was in a snit. You'd think she'd have been happy to hear how pretty she was, considering that she wasn't. But you never know with girls. Like Linda. Carlos never told her she was pretty, but she didn't mind. I mentioned it once, when we were in the hallway together. She was coming out of the bathroom and I was waiting to go in, and we kind of had to squeeze past each other.

"Carlos never says you're pretty," I said. "But you are."

"Oh, I don't mind," she said, going all squirrelly and brushing past me. Carlos was my friend first, from when we were kids. His parents had the big dairy farm across the road. That was before they sold it off and someone came in and set up a giant hog production. No wonder I left. Anyway, he married Linda. She taught kindergarten, and you could sort of see it, with her sweet voice. It got singsongy when she was talking to you.

So you just don't know.

"I saw the hair hat man again," I said.

"Really," said Linda. She was drinking a glass of orange juice and didn't want any macaronis yet because it was too early for supper. Also, she was going to broil fish for herself and didn't want to spoil her appetite.

"Who cares about your thighs," said Carlos. I looked at Linda's thighs and didn't see anything.

"He was in the park. I thought I'd go up and talk to him, only I was busy weeding the geranium patch, and when I looked up again, he was gone," I said.

"Really," said Linda. Carlos was eating a spoonful of macaroni out of the pan and not paying attention.

Actually, no. I hadn't seen him.

But I wished I had.

When I first saw him, I wasn't sure it was true. I saw him through the window of a coffee shop as I was passing by, and afterward I wished that I'd stopped and gone in, maybe gone up behind him, maybe said something.

I started going to that coffee shop. It wasn't even near my place, but I had to go somewhere to get coffee, so why not there. The lady behind the counter started to know me, I went so often.

"Large double double?" she would say.

And I would smile and say yes and how's your day going and leave the six cents left over as a tip. Not a great tip, admittedly, but six cents every day for five months must start to add up. I didn't bother doing the math, but it seemed like it might wind up being something.

She was a big girl, hefty. No one would call her pretty, but she looked like it never bothered her much. She kept her uniform clean and she brushed her hair off her face into a bun, which is how all my aunts wore their hair, and she smiled a lot, which was nice.

But the guy never showed up. I even changed the time I went, but nothing.

"Too bad you didn't get to talk to him," said Linda.

"Oh, I know," I said.

"I'm so curious," said Linda.

"Curious about what?" said Carlos.

"The man with the hair hat," said Linda.

"Oh, that," he said.

"Weren't you even paying attention?" said Linda.

Carlos didn't say anything. I didn't blame him, because who wants to be nagged at, but still, Linda had a point. She looked at him something fierce, and you know, come to think of it, Carlos didn't pay attention a lot of the time, even to me. We'd be out getting wings and watching the hockey, and I'd say something, and he'd go uh-huh, uh-huh, and you'd just know he hadn't heard a thing. He gets this blank look in his eyes and he's nodding away, but you can see he's watching the commercial instead. It could get on your nerves.

"Next time, you've got to say something," said Linda, swinging around toward me.

"Huh?" I said.

"Next time, talk to him," said Linda. "It's so curious."

"So, Carlos, do you want to do something tonight?" I said.

And he looked at Linda, a quick, not-so-nice look, and said, "Dunno," and shrugged.

"Is something going on here?" I said.

Linda was looking down at her hand, inspecting the nails.

"Oh," I said. "Okay." I can take a hint.

My place is pretty small, just the bed in one room, which is about the size of the bed, actually, and then the other room has the kitchen, living room, dining room, everything. The kitchen is about three squares of linoleum in front of a counter with a hot plate on it. I get a bit crowded in there, even when it's just me, which it is about 99 percent of the time. Most of the stuff I eat is stuff you can heat up pretty quick, just open the can and go.

Linda was all about the niceties. She followed me down the stairs and held me up in the doorway saying things that didn't really matter. "The weather's been so hot," she said, for example. And, "How do you handle the heat, working outdoors all day?" That sort of thing.

"See you 'round," I said, and she leaned out over me and wrapped her arms around my neck. It was a very friendly goodbye hug. She's friendly, but that was especially friendly, and no reason for it as I could see.

The place felt pretty lonely after walking home. I wasn't done thinking about the hug when it was time for bed, so I hoped I would dream about it, but nothing. The next morning, all I could remember was some dream about climbing a hill on my hands and knees, very boring, over and over again.

The boss called me into his office. "We're moving you to another shift," he said. "You're going to work with Tino."

"What the hell is that about," I said. "Tino should have been fired years ago."

"You and him both," said the boss, whatever that was supposed to mean. I'd only had this job for a year. Tino was about fifty years old and dog-lazy. He was always holding his lower back and making faces, like I was supposed to feel sympathetic. I mean, it's the kind of job where you need to bend over sometimes, and if you can't do that, find another line of work, buddy.

"And I don't want any more complaints about you," said the boss.

"Complaints?" I said. "Who's been complaining?"

"It's not my business to say who. Let's just say that some of your comments might have come across the wrong way, and we don't want a suit on our hands," he said.

"What do you mean 'suit'?" I said.

"Harassment," he said. "Sexual."

"You know," I said, "she's not even pretty. It was nice of me to even mention that she was pretty, seeing as she's not."

"That's the sort of comment you should keep to yourself."

This new shift kind of screwed up my day. It was in the afternoons, which meant that I had to make a special trip out in the mornings to get the coffee, and it was in a different park and not a nice one. This one had a bunch of druggies and loonies in it, camped out all over the place. Nice.

"Better wear gloves if you're going to be touching that stuff," I said to Tino, but he just puts his hand on his lower back and picks up the needle bare-handed, then he waves it around at me.

"Don't be such a dickhead," I said, but it's not like you want to play around with that stuff. I kept my distance and watched my back. Tino was turning out to be a bit of a scary guy, to tell the truth.

I was telling Linda and Carlos about him when I was over at their place. Summer was over. Linda had just started back with teaching kindergarten, and she was wearing her teaching outfit. It was blue with white around the edges, very nice, like what a kindergarten teacher should look like. We were sitting in their living room on the futon couch.

"The kids are quite rough this year," she said. "Half of them don't have parents."

"Really?" I said.

"Well, they've got someone, just not both parents."

"Oh," I said. I'd been picturing a bunch of orphans, which would really be sad.

Carlos was in the kitchen doing the dishes.

"So this Tino guy is pretty scary," I said. "He's pretty big for an old guy, and I think he might be a bit of a wacko." I didn't tell about the needle, though, because Linda looked sort of worried as it was.

"Do you think he might do something?" she said. "Should he really be working for the city?"

"Ah, he won't do anything."

"Have you seen that man with the hair hat again?" said Linda.

"Funny you should mention him," I said. "He was on the street in front of me on my way over here. But I never caught up."

"How did you know it was him?"

"He's very tall. And I've seen him before, so I knew."

"Couldn't it just have been someone wearing a hat?" she said.

"I don't think so," I said. "Don't you believe me?"

"What's this?" said Carlos, coming in from the kitchen, wiping his hands on his pants. He looked at Linda and I was looking at him, so I couldn't see what Linda was looking like, but it must have been funny, because then Carlos looked at me funny. "What's all this?"

"Nothing," I said.

"The hair hat man," said Linda right away, at the same time.

"Oh," said Carlos. "Who cares."

The lady in the coffee shop did. She was so nice for five months that I finally said something.

"You serve the best coffee in town," I said.

"Starbucks is better," she said. "But we're not bad."

"No," I said. "I mean you. You personally. You serve the nicest coffee around."

She might have been blushing, but I couldn't see because she was turned the other way to get the cream. I could see one half of her face in the mirror behind the counter, and her ear, and it looked a bit pink, but she was quite normal-looking when she brought me the coffee. "That's a kind thing to say," she said. "Most customers don't think twice about it."

"I'm not most customers," I said.

Little did she know. I had to walk five city blocks to pick up a cup of coffee and then walk all the way back to my place, by which time the coffee was pretty much cold and I'd have to heat it up again on the hot plate. That's the sort of thing you learn from experience not to mention, though.

"Have you ever," I said. "Have you ever seen a guy here," I said. "Have you ever seen a guy in here with a hair hat?" I said.

"Oh, yes," she said. "He's my boyfriend." And she laughed.

"Really?" I said.

"Yes," she said and went dead serious, and her face got a nasty shade of pink.

I didn't know, maybe it was true. "Why does he do it?" I said.

"Do what?" she said.

"Hair hat," I said. "Make his hair into a hat."

"It suits him," she said.

"You're making this up," I said. "You don't even know who I'm talking about."

The people behind me were coughing and shuffling their feet on the ground. "Next, please," she said.

I kept the six cents that day.

Linda followed me down the stairs again. Her heels clicked like tap-dancing shoes on the steps. "It's nice to see you again," she said. This time she didn't give me the big hug, just held on to my hand and patted it. "You're a nice person, you know. You should get yourself a nice girlfriend to look after you."

No shit, I'm thinking. Like that was something you should say to a guy who works all afternoon in a park with some guy named Tino and lives in a place the size of a tea bag. It just so happens that I don't have a lot of luck with the ladies. Carlos knew that. He would have known better than to say anything, but trust Linda.

"Okay," I said, trying to say it agreeably. I mean, it was nice of her to be looking out for me.

I booked Tuesday off. They didn't care that much. I never took a day off, not even one sick day.

"What's up?" said the boss. "Why Tuesday?"

"Why not?" I said. "Not your business anyhow." He was always poking his nose into business that wasn't his to mind. I'd told him about Tino, and he said, oh yes, he'd look into it, and you can bet he never did. That was the sort of business he should be worrying about, not what I was doing on Tuesday.

Tuesday, I found a quiet spot across from the coffee shop, on a bench sitting kitty-corner. I went and got my coffee like usual. The lady behind the counter said hi, just like she always did, just like we'd never had that chat the week before. I mentioned before that she wasn't that pretty, but it was an understatement. She was the size of a house, now that I looked at her. I didn't think she'd ever had a boyfriend, let alone now, let alone the actual guy I'd been looking for all these months.

I waited till about two o'clock that afternoon, and boy did I need to use the washroom by then. That coffee went straight through me, but I had to sit like nothing was bothering me, tapping my foot on the ground, shaking my knee. I didn't want to miss her, and besides, the only place to go would have been back inside the coffee shop and I didn't want her to see me again. She might guess something was up.

Just after two o'clock, there she was, opening the door, blinking in the sunlight. She wasn't wearing the uniform any more, just whatever she had on underneath, which was a big white T-shirt with a cartoon mouse on it and big black stretch pants. She had a purse swinging under her arm like a little rat on a leash. She was that big. She went down this street, right past my bench, and crossed over, then into that nice park. I never worked that park, but it sure is a nice one, lots of trees, and this big statue of a man on a horse.

The lady sat down on a bench, opened her purse, and took out a bag with a cookie in it. I'm dying by this point. I'm practically ready to haul out and go behind a tree. She eats the cookie with these slow, big chomps, crumbs all down her front. I'm hopping from one leg to the other.

That's when I spot him. The guy with the hair hat. I spot him from all the way across the park. He gets closer and closer, and I can't believe my eyes. It's really the guy. I turn around like Linda might be standing beside me and I can point him out and say, "Look it's him. He's really real." I'm turned around for about half a second, and when I turn back, I can't see him.

Jesus Murphy, I thought. I don't believe this. How much bad luck can one guy have?

Then I spotted him again. He was sitting beside the lady from the coffee shop. She was handing him a cookie. I was close enough to see the cookie, chocolate chip, and the hat, and it wasn't a hat—it was attached to his head, it was growing out of his head. No one else noticed. Everyone just kept walking by, walking by.

Not me. I started walking over to them. My feet were pulling me along. I got right up behind them and could have put my hand on his hair, but that seemed too weird. So I walked around the bench, as if I were just passing by, and did this sort of double take.

"Is that you?" I said to the lady. "The lady from the coffee shop?"

"Oh," she said. "Yah, I recognize you."

"Is that your boyfriend?" I said. Maybe I was pointing. I don't remember.

"It isn't polite to point," she said.

"Is that hair real?" I said. Which was a dumb question, you have to admit. Of all the questions I could have opened with, that was not the best that comes to mind.

"What, this?" said the man, and he put his hand on his head. He smiled to himself.

"It's shaped like a hat," I said.

"Oh," he said. "That's right." Just like I'd said it was a nice day and he was agreeing.

"What's up with that?" I said.

"Nothing," he said, and he leaned over the lady and brushed a few crumbs off her chest. Right in front of me.

Like I need to see a guy with hair for a hat rubbing crumbs off the enormous bosoms of his lady friend.

"Hey, Carlos, are you there? Hey, Linda, are you there?" I knocked on the door to their place. I knocked and knocked, and then I started to pound a little harder. I was kind of worried that something might be wrong. I hadn't heard from them in a while, and no one had been answering the phone.

"Knock it off already," said this guy from the next place over. He pushed up the window and leaned out to shout at me.

"I'm just trying to see my friends," I said. "They're not answering."

"Who?" said the guy. "That guy and that girl?"

"Yah," I said.

"They're gone," he said.

"What?" I said. What would this guy know anyway. "Gone where?"

"Moved or something. Don't ask me. They had a truck loaded up. So knock it off with the hammering already or I'll call the cops."

That wasn't hammering. He doesn't know hammering. If I wanted to hammer, I'd hammer and he'd know hammering.

"What do you know anyway?" I said. But I said it to the sidewalk because he'd already banged down the window. I said it to the sidewalk and then I said it to the door, and then I stopped saying it because it didn't make much sense to stand there saying things to myself when I needed a pee that badly. I almost wondered whether I'd make it home.

FLIRTATIONS

"WHY DO WE have to go to this thing?" said James.

"You don't have to go. You don't have to do anything," I said. "You can sit here on the couch and watch hockey in your underwear." For all I care, I did not add.

"Maybe I will."

"Grand. Great. Do."

"Those people are awful, you know. Awful."

"I'm one of those people."

"Not you."

"Whatever you want to do, do." I brushed my hair until it shone and applied pale green eyeshadow in the bathroom mirror. James watched from the doorway. He was actually in his underwear and a pair of black socks. He'd just driven home along a treacherous highway and angry city streets from a day of hard, honest work. I'd slept in till ten, made myself a tuna mac casserole for lunch, read on the couch and fallen briefly asleep, and for penance walked down the street to return three books to the Victoria College library. On the way home, I'd stopped at the convenience store to buy a can of root beer. It was my latest indulgence. I sucked back the brown syrup while playing Minesweeper on my computer. Needless to say, I had a final paper due in a week. The Minesweeper was supposed to warm up my brain, while the root beer fuelled it. Evening threatened to arrive, and I hastily wrote three sentences that might later prove brilliant; or not.

It had taken me two years to figure out that when James said he did not care if I slept all day, he meant it. As long as you're happy, it's not my problem, he said. Still, I reported the possibly brilliant sentences to him when he walked in the door. "I think I'm finally getting at the thesis. I think I'm getting close."

He was hungry, but I said we could eat at the party.

"What kind of food will they have?"

"Bar food, probably. Nachos and wings. Maybe pizza."

"Why do we have to go to this thing?"

I slicked dark red on my lips and admired the effect. "How does this look?"

"Fine."

"Fine? That's all? Just fine?"

Silence. I was developing a notion that I would prefer to go to the party alone.

"I'll get dressed," said James, dragging himself down the hallway, past the plants, which flourished outrageously under a leaky skylight.

~

Do you care about these people? I thought as we climbed purple carpeted stairs to a smoky bar over Yonge Street, crammed ourselves into a shabby room reserved by the Graduate English Association.

"Is that the food?" said James, pointing to a plate of ravished nachos, the remainder stuck together in a soggy lump.

"Why don't you just order something yourself?"

"What would you like?"

"Oh, nothing. I'm fine."

"Nothing to drink?"

"Just a gin and tonic, maybe."

People hugged the perimeter like contestants at a wallflower ball. They clutched at glasses of beer or spirit and squashed napkins into their palms, their faces politely strained. We're trying, their expressions said. We came out.

I edged closer to a boy from Eighteenth-Century Poetry, the one who could bullshit his way out of a paper bag, the one with the glasses and the bald spot. "Hey there," I said.

"Hey," he said.

I liked him quite a lot. He was, if I admitted it to myself, the reason I had come tonight. Maybe, maybe, was the thought beating in my head. Maybe he will be there. He had an ordinary name I no longer recall; I shall call him Scott for convenience.

There had been a brief, brave moment in Eighteenth-Century Poetry when it had seemed that Scott had liked me too. After my presentation on Lady Mary Wortley Montagu, he said it was the best he'd heard so far. Would I like to get together sometime?

Oh yes, I said. That would be great. Oh yes, I said, thinking to myself, This is not a date. This is a friendly meeting of the minds. I pretended he was gay—he was slender, witty—and that soothed my conscience. I might even have told James about the gay friend I had made at school, how we were meeting for a drink.

We went to a bar on campus after class and told each other vague life stories, bragged a bit, drank more than was prudent for an outing in broad daylight. Then he called me at home and set my heart yammering, and that I could not afford. You see, I had intended for everything to be innocent, and it was; and it was not. I liked him more than was wise to admit.

On our next outing, I confessed.

"So that's who answered the phone?" he said.

"Yes," I had to say, lowering my head in something that was not shame because it was too close to regret.

That was the end of that.

"Hey there," I said to him in the dank bar. Out the windows beyond his head was Yonge Street, looking greasy and beleaguered.

Scott was half turned against me, watching out of the corner of his eye a young woman with short dark hair and a nose ring, attractive in a punk rock grrrl vein, not the type I would have associated with Scott's humorous diatribes on Marshall McLuhan. She laughed up at the ceiling, a laugh of long familiarity and inside jokes, and turned away from me. I saw they were holding hands.

"What's up?" he said. It had been months since we'd seen each other. He looked as if time had not passed more pleasantly, more breezily, than in those months.

"Not much," I said, casting about for an anecdote.

"Right," he said. The pair of them found a way to move in another direction, like salmon spawning.

Here is the truth about our meetings: they meant more to me than to him. My hand prickled as it lay next to his, not quite touching, on the table in our classroom. In the margins of my notes on poor crippled Pope were scrawled mention of these hands and the blond hair sprouting from the knuckles.

When I told him about James, it imploded in an instant.

"So that's—" he said.

"Yah," I said, as if I were talking about the weather. We were sitting in an empty courtyard on a stone wall. All around us leaves were falling, brilliant orange and yellow, onto clipped grass. Our hands were placed decorously side by side.

"Okay," he said.

Just then, as if called down from the heavens, a flock of birds swooped into our courtyard and straight at us. Small black birds, their wings rustling, their voices calling. They parted around us, dozens of them, hundreds, a sea of shiny feathers and bird cries.

It was the single most gorgeous moment in my life, a moment of insanity, unscripted, unforeseen, the wings opening and closing around us, brushing our flesh. Then they were gone. We looked at each other in wonderment. Nothing like that had ever happened to me before, or since. It seemed that we had been christened by the birds, blessed, that we should therefore fall together.

If he thought anything of the sort, he did not reveal it.

"So that's who answered the phone," he said.

"Yes," I said. I wanted to talk about the birds, but I did not have the courage, or folly, to say what I meant, what I felt.

James was at my elbow with a gin and tonic. "Who was that?" he said. His first pint was down to the dregs, and he balanced a second on the windowsill behind us.

"Oh, nobody. Just someone from a class last fall."

For days after the birds, I felt something akin to disgust whenever James came to touch me. We spent that Friday night driving all over the north of Toronto in a rented van looking for a burger place James remembered eating at once. I sat beside him frozen with irritation, and disappointment, as if I'd missed my train and had to take the bus instead.

James said later it was the most fun he'd had in a while.

We found the burger place. We ate in a booth, our burgers freshly made and placed in little red baskets with curly fries. I looked across the table and saw his face, relaxed over the sandwich, broad in the forehead, as familiar as a loaf of bread. I did not know what to say to him.

"Are you going to cruise around? Talk to some people?" said James, starting the second pint. He had perked up.

"Yes," I said.

"I ordered the fish and chips."

I stared around the room, sparing myself nothing. Nobody was especially ugly here. Nobody was especially beautiful. The fashion was conservative. The hairstyles unflattering.

"Who's that guy?" said James. "What a dork."

"That's the president of the association."

"What a dork."

"You already said that."

The president was screwing together his own personal pool cue, which came in a black leather carrying case. His belly bulged over a pair of tan pants, and he set a glass of pale beer on a nearby table. "Who wants to challenge me? Anybody? Any of you master's students want to get your asses kicked?" His voice graced the higher octaves, thin as a stick, breathy.

"Jesus," said James.

"Don't laugh at him," I said.

The president chalked up his cue with a swagger and broke. It was a truly godawful shot. The cue ball leapt off the table and rolled about the floor. The others remained in a perfect triangle at the far end, untouched. The president did not seem to notice. “Throw me that ball,” he said loudly, and then he cued up again. This time, the black ball shot into the corner pocket.

“That’s the game,” said his challenger.

“I think not,” said the president. “I think not. I’m just warming up. Who’s next?”

“Who does that guy think he is?” said James. He was from the real world. They flay such people in the real world.

“Fish and chips?” shouted the waitress, in black shoes, black pants, black shirt. She waved an oversized plate aggressively. The room was packed, and everyone avoided looking at her.

“Honey,” I said. “That’s probably you.”

“Over here,” said James. He slipped her an extra five dollars, and she gave him a wink.

“Hey, big spender,” I said.

James moved toward a table in the corner. “These fuckers probably tip worth shit,” he said.

“You get mean when you drink,” I said, tagging after him.

He affected not to hear me. The table was occupied, but it had a vacant chair.

“Go ahead,” said the man sitting there. He wore a hat.

“Thanks,” said James.

"I'll just be over there," I said. I'd finished my gin and tonic. The man with the hat did not look like a student. He was old, by my standards, probably nearing fifty. It was hard to see in the dark. What I noticed about him was that the smallest fingernail on his left hand was painted pink. The lighting was dim, but it stood out.

I hunched under a row of mirrors and rested the small of my back against the wall's decorative padding. Plastic, not leather. I did not know many people, and the thought depressed me. I had spent nearly a year with this group, and they were strangers. When I moved to Toronto, it had been a big leap, a "pivotal choice," as Dr. Phil would say. None of these people watch "Oprah," I thought. None of them read Agatha Christie. They're busy with their Foucault, their Derrida, their Roland bloody Barthes.

I was pretty, but I was not smart enough. I needed to be two inches smarter. I needed to be able to talk about conceits without sounding lost. Even now, standing under the mirrors, I could not remember how a conceit worked, what it meant. Use it in a sentence, I thought.

Across the room, James patiently devoured his fish and chips. I saw his jaw working. He was nodding and smiling as the man in the hat talked. James waved down the waitress, and I saw his lips move, his teeth flash, a laugh. I imagined him saying, "Another pint, please. And one for my friend."

Use it in a sentence, I thought. Not conceited. Conceit.

"Excuse me," said the man beside me. He had not been beside me when I came over to the wall but had worked his way around and through people. I had seen him coming. What the hell, I thought.

"Yes?" I said.

"You could use another drink. What are you having?"

"Oh. Gin and tonic, I guess."

"Wait here," he said. He had an English accent and wore a pleasant sweater, not hairy, not tweedy, not Christmasy; somehow manly. That is something you cannot often say about sweaters.

"Here we are," he said, reappearing with a drink. "I got you a double."

"That's awfully nice."

"You looked all alone."

"I'm not. It's just . . ."

"These people," he said. "I don't know why I came out. I don't know anyone."

"I know."

"And who would want to."

Our eyes trailed in tandem to the middle of the room, where the president was hooting with glee and stabbing the air with his pool cue. The man beside me smiled wickedly. He had a face that would not be kind: narrow, sardonic. I liked it.

"What are you studying?" he said.

"I'm not sure I can bear to talk about it."

"You're doing a doctorate?"

"Oh God, no. I'm just a master's."

"What's wrong with that?"

"Nothing."

"Who cares what you're doing."

"It's very hierarchical here, don't you find?"

"Oh that. Who gives a shit?"

His name was Julian. He was writing a doctoral thesis on someone I'd never heard of. He was the sort of person I could admit this to.

"Nobody's heard of him," he said. "You've got beautiful hair."

Across the room, James looked up and at me, lifted three fingers in a small salute. He had finished his fish and chips and was relaxed, content. A fresh pint reposed by his elbow. Julian was facing me and did not see. I noticed that his arm rested comfortably on the wall beside my shoulder. It seemed the double had gone down rather easily.

"You'll want another," said Julian. "Wait for me."

The room went swimmingly around us as we leaned together through the haze of smoke and alcohol. You know how a room changes as you change. The walls and ceiling hang lower. The air is darker: it cloaks you and your companion as you shout into the other's ear and lips brush hair. His hand moves to your upper arm as he makes a point, and it does not move away. Somehow, it feels quite natural, because the room has become so heavy, that his hand should stay there on your arm, the fingers rubbing up and down ever so slightly, the heat and pressure.

"I have to tell you," I said. "I came with someone."

"Oh, that's all right," said Julian, his hand slipping down to my elbow.

"In fact," I said, "I live with him."

"Me too," said Julian. "I live with a girl too."

"We have so much in common."

"She's possibly crazy. I couldn't leave her. She gets suicidal."

"And you love her."

"I do." His face, next to mine, fell into seriousness like a curtain falling to the stage.

"I love mine too," I said.

We laughed easily. We were joyful. I saw his teeth just before he kissed me on the temple.

"Hmm," I said. "Perhaps we shouldn't."

"So sorry," he said, drawing back. "I can't say what came over me."

James floated into my line of sight. If he had seen, his face had not altered to register it. The man with the hat had been joined by a woman who dwarfed the chair she sat on, her buttocks swelling over the seat, consuming it. She's not a student, I thought. Definitely not. They're not supposed to be here. James laughed with his head thrown back. I could hear it all the way across the noisy room. It was his salesman laugh: from the back of the throat, harsh, like gunfire.

"Did it come over you too?" said Julian. I had forgotten Julian.

"I'm sorry?" I said.

"The moment," he said. "The overcoming of it. The thing that spontaneously occurred."

"Oh," I said. I was not thinking clearly. I wanted to go to James and tell him not to laugh like that. It stood out in the room. It made a fool of him.

"We're off," said Scott. I could not make out his face, even though it hovered next to my left ear.

"See you later," I said, although I did not understand why he was addressing me.

"No introductions?" said Scott. I saw that I still liked his eyes. I looked down. I still liked his hands too. One rested casually on my sleeve.

"Pardon?" I said.

"Won't you introduce me to your boyfriend?" he said, nodding at Julian.

"Right," I said. "That's not him."

"That's not him?"

"No."

"But I saw—"

"He's here. I don't know where he is, that's all."

Julian stood through this all, smiling vaguely to himself in the mirror. Scott's face was pale, affectionate, confused.

"This is Julian. He's a doctoral candidate," I said. "Julian, this is Scott."

"A pleasure," said Julian.

"Likewise," said Scott, eyeing me with puzzlement, but I turned myself into a wall of ignorance. "Well, we're off."

The girl behind him had melted and shrunk, and he walked past her as if she were not there. She had to chase after him. I thought to myself, So he did like me back. But it did not matter much. I did not, at that moment, think about the birds.

"You're a doll," said Julian. Was he still here? I did not want him. The air in the room had grown stale, sickening. I was nauseated, and he was not the person I wished to confess this to.

It was snowing unexpectedly when we stumbled into the street.

"What the hell," said James. "What the hell when it's already spring."

"I love it," I said. Fat flakes brushed my nose, cooled my skin. When I threw my head back to see them crowding the sky, I got dizzy. "Oh no."

"You'll be okay. Just keep moving."

"I can't," I said thickly. "I'm sorry."

"Just keep your feet moving like this." James took me by the elbows. I was encircled by his particular smell. It always reminded me of vinegar and apple juice. "I was thinking about the marriage thing again," he said.

My eyes were closed, head hanging, as I lifted one foot, then the other. "Why?" I said sadly. "Why now?"

"I've been thinking about it for a while," he said. He wanted to make an honest woman of me, that seemed to be the shape of it. I was fighting an inner buzzing and could not concentrate properly.

"No," I said, "no." My eyes flung open as a car without a muffler roared by. I stumbled into a narrow alley, but the truth is I would have thrown up anywhere. At times like these, you are without shame. You have earned the vomit splattering your shoes and the hem of your trousers.

James waited nearby. He knew better than to touch me. "You're okay," I heard him saying over and over, and I would be. I was.

"I'm drunk," I said finally, wiping my mouth with the back of my hand, then wiping my hands on my pants. "I hate being drunk."

"Would you like to get married?" he said.

I was still spitting, one hand pressed weakly against the black painted wall adorned with white graffiti. I squinted at an illegible tag spread across the brick like a flattened pair of wings and wondered what it meant.

"That man kept asking me, 'Do you care? Do you care that your girlfriend is flirting with someone else?'" James waited for me to be done spitting.

"How did he know?" I said, pushing upright. I could not look at him.

"I told him who you were."

"You did?" I was ashamed, thinking of what had been on display.

"I said, 'Why be jealous? She's coming home with me.'"

We paused. I looked at him then. "That's true," I said. I stepped onto the sidewalk bathed in artificial light.

"He said he was very jealous. He was very suspicious of his girlfriend."

"Who? That fat lady?" We began walking for home.

"You saw."

"I watch what you're doing too," I said. We could not stop looking now, throwing glances back and forth, although the sidewalk was busy and people pressed to pass. He took my hand formally, and our fingers laced together. Each glance was kind. It was truthful.

"It's just flirting," I said.

"I know," said James. He would wait outside our bathroom for me as I brushed my teeth and washed the pretty remains of lipstick and green eyeshadow off my face. He would not flatter me; he never would. He would stroke the skin of my back beneath the covers until I fell asleep. He would not be disgusted by anything I said or did; he would not buy it. In the morning, he would go for the paper and takeout coffee while I lay sleeping. If ever he dreamed of fat ladies, he would not tell.

This was not a list of pros and cons. These were not the only reasons I would marry him, someday, when the time called us to it.

THE APARTMENT

I HAD A HEADACHE. It had started in the morning, not long after the girl downstairs, Kelly, left for work. I was outside in my poncho, digging up the glad bulbs for next season, when she appeared, dressed head to toe in black and carrying a brown leather bag.

"You look so nice today, Kelly," I said.

She slapped on a smile but didn't slow down. "Good morning, Mrs. Thanos."

"Oh wait, oh, Kelly," I said. "Kelly, it's the day for recycling. I saw you had cans piled up. Today is the day."

She scowled. "Jonathan took them out this morning."

"But they're not in the bin."

"Yes, they are," she said. "He took them out. They're not in the apartment any more."

"But I checked our bin. They're not there."

"Well, they're gone from our place, so they must be somewhere." She was not a friendly girl. It was always rush, rush, rush.

"Oh," I said. "Well, they must be somewhere if they're not there. I just wanted to check. I saw you had cans piled up. That was all."

"Well, goodbye, Mrs. Thanos. I'm late for the bus."

My daughter told me to leave the young couple alone. "Don't bother them. We need the rent," said Yalta.

The rent. This is what happens when you take out a second mortgage to send your daughter to the university and then your husband dies.

"I paid you back, Mother," said Yalta. "I paid you back for university, and you put it back into the house. That was years ago. The house is paid off." My daughter worked in the financial industry. That was how she put it. I called a secretary a secretary.

"Then why do we need these boarders?"

"There are taxes," she said. "Also, the roof leaks or the window breaks. Or we need to buy a new washing machine. And they're not boarders. They're tenants."

Yalta was the younger of my two girls, and the prettier, although none of us was handsome. When we looked in the mirror, the mirror had a good laugh. Yalta pranced around the attic apartment in a flowing green skirt like a hippie, hair to her waist, pretending she was not over forty.

"Your eggs are not getting any younger," I said to her.

"I won't dignify that with a comment," she said. That was a favourite phrase of hers.

I had a headache. It came on with a dull pounding, like a blood pudding pushing into the sides of my skull, not long after Kelly had walked around the corner to catch her bus. "Have a nice day, Kelly," I called, but she shrugged. It was hardly a wave. The glad bulbs were tucked into a brown paper bag, and I left them on the porch steps. From inside my poncho I drew out a key.

"Stop going in there," said Yalta. "They are tenants. The apartment belongs to them."

This was foolishness.

"Have you seen the kitchen?" I said to Yalta. "You would think she never sweeps."

"Maybe she doesn't," said Yalta. "But they're better than the last one, remember? He never did his dishes, and the pizza boxes everywhere."

The key fit neatly into the lock and turned with a click, soft as a footstep. Kelly had been telling the truth: the cans were gone. But they were piled up and spilling out of the bin yesterday, and I checked our bin this morning. It had nothing but our cans. What had Jonathan done with them? This would be the sort of question Yalta would discourage me from asking.

"You telling me what to do," I said. I had seen two different men leaving her rooms under cover of darkness, early in the morning; two men in one month. One never came back again. What did that mean? I asked her. Was it a one-night stand?

"Oh, Mother. I am completely and utterly grown up."

"Then act like it," I said.

"If I moved out, what would you do?"

"That's not what I meant, silly girl. You only hear what you want to hear."

The other man was everywhere, like a bad rash, springing up when you least expect. He popped out of the woodwork on the stairs, which was not good for my weak heart.

"Hello, Mrs. Thanos," he mumbled. Not much of a way of speaking.

I could not remember his name, although Yalta told it to me again and again. "Hello. And how are you?"

"Oh, very well, Mrs. Thanos." He had a bad habit of rubbing his nose under the bridge of his eyeglasses, which did not improve his looks. When I mentioned this to Yalta, she sighed heavily.

"Have you seen me recently, Mother? I'm not exactly a supermodel."

The downstairs was so nice and so quiet, with a stream of sunlight coming through the stained glass above the front window. There was no stained glass in the windows in my rooms. I wondered whether Kelly and Jonathan ever stopped to look at the colours. There was a shade of purple that made me think of a dusty road I walked along as a girl, on the way to school. I did not like school, not like Yalta. It frightened and bored me all at once. That was not in this country.

When we came to Canada, I would have been happy with a larger yard for my garden. My husband did not wish to disappoint me. "It is small, but I can find room for my tomatoes," I said to him.

"I knew you could make it work," he said.

"What else do you expect?" I said.

In the evening, my husband took off his shoes and put on his slippers and sat in my garden. He smoked his cigarettes, and I watched him through the kitchen window while I scrubbed the supper dishes. Every so often, he turned around in his chair and waved at me.

Kelly had not swept in some time. Without even straining my eyes or bending over, I could see fat piles of fluff and dirt under the rocking chair and the television stand. There was a funny smell in the air, which I could not place. It was like a vegetable left out on the counter and going to rot, although I saw nothing there. The garbage bin under the sink was empty too. The door to their bedroom was open, the bed made. This I would say for Kelly: she did the dishes and she made the bed every day. She tried. She did work very hard, going out early in the morning and coming home late, with her husband. They had no life that I could see. Work, eat in front of the television, sleep. On the weekends, they came home very late, drunk as stink.

"Let's order a pizza," Jonathan would say. The walls and floors were thin.

"I think I'll be sick," Kelly would say.

The shower curtain was in a state. Perhaps Kelly did not know it should be washed once a month. I would not want to interfere, but Yalta and I had gone shopping for it together, and we hung it ourselves before Kelly and Jonathan moved in. A pretty yellow colour to match the blue tiles.

Perhaps I will call Kelly and leave her a message about this shower curtain, I said to myself, then I froze.

There was a click, the soft click of the key in the door to this apartment. Footsteps, floorboards creaking, a sigh, a muttered "dammit," rustling from the living room. I was paralyzed behind the bathroom door. My headache began thumping and pumping like a gymnast. I caught myself in the mirror, a ghastly sight with grey whiskers sprouting above pinched lips, a face you would not want to run into in the dark. The bathroom door was half open, and I was pressed up against the sink, my hip worrying the porcelain. Despite the darkness, I could see that Kelly had not rinsed the tub recently. The mirror was dusty and spotted. These were mine too, although Yalta would advise me not to mention it.

"Why call it advice when you're just ordering an old woman around."

"Don't be petulant, for God's sake."

"Why do you go around swearing like that? It would break your father's heart."

"Can we stop bickering, please? I'm expecting Gordon"—or Jeremy, or Richard, or Michael; whatever his name was—"any minute."

Steps came into the kitchen. A cough.

"Where is it?" A rustling, then a flinging of drawers and doors open and shut. Kelly pushed against the bathroom door, switched the light on and off, barely sticking her head in. "This is so not worth it. You're going to be late again," she said. It was nice to hear someone else address themselves like that, in private. It was not so nice to be pressed farther into a sink in a dark bathroom that someone else might consider theirs.

The footsteps receded. The door slammed shut and there was silence. I heard my heart pounding, and that was when the headache really struck. I could barely drag myself out the door, and only hours later, when I woke up from a nap on my couch, would I reach into the pocket of my poncho and realize the key was gone.

Yalta was knocking on the door. "Mother, are you available? I'd like to talk to you."

The key was gone. I searched both pockets and tried to rid my head of cobwebs.

"Mother? It's not urgent, but it's relatively important."

I had not had my cup of tea this morning. That might explain such terrible clumsiness, but perhaps it was a sign of something much worse, something my daughters had been hinting at for some time now.

"Mother, are you all right in there?"

"Yes, Yalta. I am fine."

"May I come in, then?"

"Please, come in."

"Let me make you some tea," said Yalta.

"You are home early," I said.

"No," she said. "I always work half days on Wednesdays."

"You do," I said. "Of course."

"You look flustered."

"I was pulling the glad bulbs this morning."

"I saw. You left the bag on the steps. Michael"—or Gordon, or Richard, or Jeremy—"tripped over them leaving the house."

"What was he doing leaving the house at such an hour?"

"I told you, Mother, we're quite serious about each other. That's what I wanted to talk to you about."

"You don't need my permission to marry. You're old enough."

"Oh, Jesus," said Yalta. "We don't want to get married."

"It's a sin and a shame," I said.

"Not these days," she said.

"Have you made the tea yet? My head aches something dreadful."

"It's steeping," she said. "Mother, Richard"—or Jeremy, or Michael, or Gordon—"has asked me to move in with him, and I suggested that he move in with me instead. Here."

"Here."

"Well, what would you do if I moved out, Mother."

"I just said, 'Here.' I didn't say anything."

"We don't want to be in your way. It just seemed to make sense. He's here most nights anyway."

"That I do not need to hear about."

The tea passed into my stomach like poison and gave me gas. The thought of being sandwiched between couples, the young ones down and the old ones up, affected me poorly. After Yalta left, blushing an unbecoming purple, I went and scrubbed the lower cupboards in the kitchen until my hands were raw as hamburger. The key. I could see it shining on the ledge of the bathroom sink. My way in and my way out. I did not have another. Yalta would, but I could not drag Yalta into this.

The doorbell rang and rang. "Yalta," I shouted, until my head only hurt more.

It was a man in a hat. "Is Ms. Thanos in?" he said.

"Do you mean me?"

"The Ms. Thanos I'm looking for is somewhat younger," he said.

"And who are you?"

He was older than Yalta, and although he looked respectable, there was something wrong about his appearance. It was his hair. That wasn't a hat—it was hair. I slammed the door shut in surprise.

The ringing of the doorbell started up again. "Go away," I said.

I felt out of sorts. I put my hand on the door to the downstairs rooms, but I could not open it.

"Stop ringing, please." I thought my head would burst.

"May I leave a message?" called the man through the door.

"No. No messages. Go away now. She is living with someone else."

"She dropped her wallet. I found it. I only wish to return it."

"I won't fall for these tricks," I said, and I started up the stairs with a heavy heart.

"I will leave it in the mailbox," he said.

The telephone waited on a walnut stand by the window. I twitched aside the blind and saw the man with the hat standing in my tulip bed. He did not know it was my tulip bed because it had been dug up and mulched for winter. Still, he could have stood on the sidewalk instead.

The man was stooped in the shoulders, too old for my Yalta. He looked to the house and raised his eyes, catching me. I moved out of sight like an old bear stumbling behind a bramble bush, but it was too late. His eyes were mean with laughter.

I would not be laughed at.

But when I yanked aside the blind again, to stare him down and send him away with something to think about, he was gone. I watched the wind blow yellow leaves up and down the street.

My hand was on the telephone, but I did not look at it. I told myself, Do not pick it up. Do not dial the number. Why stand here by the telephone and tempt yourself, I thought. There is nothing to see but dead leaves blowing. Go do something useful. But I had not the energy to trudge downstairs and continue digging in my fall garden. It would be so easy to explain. They would understand. I let the blind slip back into place.

"Hello, Kelly. This is Mrs. Thanos, Mrs. Thanos from upstairs. Kelly, I noticed that your shower curtain needs to be washed. If you would please let me do that, I would be happy, since it is my shower curtain. Please call me back. Also, there is a key that I need in your bathroom. A key to the apartment. Could you give it back to me, please? Thank you, Kelly. Call back soon."

Yalta fluttered into my rooms like an overgrown butterfly.

"Where were you, I might ask," I said, lifting my hand off the telephone like it was on fire.

"I just wanted to invite you to dinner, Mother. Would you join us upstairs?"

"The doorbell was ringing off the hook, and no one to get it."

"Doorbells can't ring off hooks. We're cooking Indian. You'll love it."

"My stomach can't take the spices."

"Who was at the door?"

"A man for you. And he had a hair hat."

"Why are you looking so accusatory? And what in God's name is a hair hat?"

"Who is this man, Yalta? What are you thinking, moving in with someone."

"Oh, very nice, Mother. You think I'm sleeping with every man I clap eyes on."

"Well, who is to say."

"We'd like to have you for dinner. I'll leave it at that."

There was no phone call, no message, nothing, when I returned from Yalta's apartment, bloated like a sick sheep from the curries and garlic. They were home. They were making a lot of noise. I turned on the dishwasher to cover it up.

"Who does she think she is?" shouted Kelly. "Fucking shower curtain, my ass."

"Please," said Jonathan, "she can probably hear you."

"I don't give a flying fuck," she screamed. "I hope she does. Fuck you, Mrs. Thanos!"

Yalta would be most unhappy if she were to catch wind of this. She would side with the newlyweds, not with me, her own mother.

I turned on the television, too, to cover the shouts. I had no wish to eavesdrop.

The telephone rang. "Hello? Mrs. Thanos? It's Jonathan from downstairs."

"Oh, Jonathan, hello. How are you?"

"Okay. Listen, Mrs. Thanos, would you mind turning off

the dishwasher? It makes a loud noise in the bedroom, and Kelly is trying to sleep. She is not feeling well."

"She is not well? What is the matter?"

"Oh, nothing. She's just a little tired from work."

"Of course, Jonathan. I will go turn off the dishwasher now." The key wavered in my mind.

"Thank you, Mrs. Thanos."

"You tell Kelly I hope she will be feeling better."

"Thank you."

"Oh, Jonathan. Jonathan. I called earlier about the key. Do you know about the key?"

"What key?"

"Just a regular key, regular size."

"Sorry," he said.

"If you see it," I said.

"Right. Goodbye, then."

With the dishwasher off, I could hear Yalta's silly giggles upstairs. She sounded like a girl of twelve. I would turn the television louder, but then Kelly might complain some more. There was nothing to be done. It was dark and I could not go into my garden. My nightgown flapped around my ankles as I wandered the rooms, belching quietly. There was too much furniture here, but I had not wished to give any of it away, or sell it, after we'd rearranged the house for the boarders. Yalta begged and pleaded, but I told her she would be happy one day, when all this would be hers.

"You barely have room to move, Mother."

"You will thank me. You and your sister both."

"Most of this stuff is worthless," said Yalta.

"Do you think your father worked his whole life for nothing?"

Each thing he bought for me, over the years, was always a surprise. "Surprise! What do you think I have brought you home this time?"

It would be a new sofa, gold velvet and tassels, or a new rug, thick and soft and covered in beautiful flowers, or the bed that Yalta slept in now, sturdy and made of fine carved maple. He was a quiet man, not one to wear his feelings on his sleeve like some.

"My father never embraced me, not even once," I heard Yalta tell this man she is now living with, her voice full of pity for herself and disbelief, as if she were saying that her father beat her or abandoned her. I was sitting in their dining room waiting for the curries and the garlic when I heard this.

"Yalta," I called. "Yalta, what are you saying?"

She did not hear me over the bubbling pots and running dishwater. I did not have the energy to call any louder. The headache was going away, leaving behind it a sadness and heaviness.

"Eat up, Mother. We've got loads."

Gordon—or Michael or Jeremy or Richard—nodded eagerly, gesturing toward the laden table and knocking over his glass of water.

"I don't have the heart for more," I said to Yalta, who was batting her eyes foolishly at this man, daubing at the table and his arms with a napkin. "My stomach is not made for these spices." What I thought I needed was to be in my nightgown and slippers, in my own rooms.

But this did not satisfy me. My head was limp and swollen. The key was gone, and it sat downstairs in Kelly's thin, white hand, and she would never give it up.

There was a time when I thought Kelly was a nice girl, a kind girl. We had several talks while she was doing her laundry. I would hear her going down to the basement, and I would rush down too.

"Oh, Kelly. Why you don't wash the whites with hot water? All your underthings, they need the hot water to get out the germs."

She did not know the first thing about laundry.

"Thank you, Mrs. Thanos. That sounds like good advice."

"Kelly, I am always telling Yalta how to do the washing, and she will not pay attention. I should do her laundry for her!"

"You should."

"She will not let me."

"Oh."

"Kelly, it is a good idea for you to wash the wood floors with a special kind of wax. I have some upstairs I will lend to you."

Yalta told me not to keep running down there. She told me Kelly would grow tired of our conversations, but I said Kelly was a polite girl, and not like some people. Not so easily bored. She appreciated my suggestions and thanked me for them.

My hands slipped over the dark wood of the dining-room table. I touched the backs of the chairs, the shade of the lamp in the corner glowing red, the top of the television. There was no dust anywhere. I heard the front door open and close, and I pulled back the blind. Kelly and Jonathan were walking off in the dark, hand in hand. So much for Kelly feeling sick.

I opened my door and crept down the stairs. At the bottom of the stairs, hanging on my door handle, was a plastic shopping bag. Inside was the shower curtain, a wallet, and the key. The key. It was at the very bottom of the bag, taped to a note.

Dear Mrs. Thanos, You can keep the shower curtain. We have bought our own. The wallet was in the mailbox and is not ours. We did not open it. Here is the key.

Dear children. Dear, dear children. Now I would have to say nothing to Yalta of this mistake. She would never know. The boarders returned your wallet, I would say to her. They found it in the mailbox. I would not ask her where she lost it, or why a man with a hat for hair brought it back. I would be quiet and not bother her, now that she was so happy. I could hear her laughing all the way down here, at the bottom of the stairs. It bounced off the walls and made my heavy head even heavier, because I knew what it meant. They would all be leaving me soon, even Yalta. Or I would be leaving them. It would amount to the same thing, with all the space it would leave behind, and the furniture.

The key was in my hand, and I put it into the lock and opened the door. Even at night, the stained glass glowed in beautiful colours. I stood in the middle of the room and felt, just for a moment, at home.

THIRD DOG

THE FIRST ONE came at us as we rounded the corner, pee running freely down his hind leg as he leapt from a squat on someone's lawn and burst at us with puppyish yelps. I spun the stroller around and attempted a casual air. Dogs can smell fear, I thought, but this did not help.

The dog loped across the street, looking neither right nor left, tongue lolling. He was only a puppy, but a large and wolfish one, and I feared for you, little man, strapped into that seat, toes dangling like bait. Frank would have known what to do. I stood like a raccoon in the headlights, squat, fearful, feeble. It all seemed to be happening in slow motion, the dog's jaws flailing open, the nipping paws.

"Come here, beastie," shouted a girl in men's overalls, stepping out of her house and spying the scene. She caught the dog by the collar just before he reached us. "Bad dog," she said. "He's harmless. I'm very sorry."

"That's okay," I said, feeling foolish, standing pigeon-toed on the sidewalk with the stroller half turned. Your tongue was out, I saw as I bent to straighten the blanket covering your feet. You smiled when you caught sight of my face, a bursting grin that threatened to melt my heart. We can say that, we grandmothers, if only to ourselves.

You and I were on our way to the park. Your mother was at home, making frantic phone calls to lawyers and best friends, pretending to smile at herself in all the windows she passed. I saw her touch a hand to her hair, sigh to herself blearily. She had promised she wouldn't have anything more to drink this morning. It was such a beautiful morning, I'd pointed out. That blue sky.

"I've only had a small glass of wine," she said.

"Oh, of course," I said.

"So don't be all accusing."

"Honey, of course not."

"You were giving me that look," she said, handing me the baby, you, all of four months old.

I attempted to erase anything untoward from my features.

"I wouldn't drink anything more, not with the baby to feed," she said, then she began to tear up. "How could you think that?"

"Sweetheart, I never thought that."

"Douglas thinks that," she said, as misty and dour as a November evening.

"Oh," I said. "Well, I don't know about that, of course."

"I'm sorry," she said. "I don't mean to go on like this."

"I'll just take the baby to the park," I said, "while you get some things done. Don't you worry about us."

The woman in overalls dragged the puppy across the street into her yellow brick house. There were no curtains on the windows, and we'd peeked in on previous walks: bare walls of colours you could eat—eggplant, lemon, chocolate. We saw the dog romping in the empty front room, tearing at a cushion.

"Dogs are often quite gentle creatures," I said, swinging the stroller in the direction of the park. "They are best when on the leash or chained to the porch, but on the whole, they are quite lovely animals. You will enjoy playing with them when you are older. You will pull their tails and ears."

The second loose dog was bounding through back-yards only a block away, although we could not guess that. You were very quiet. One elbow listed out the side of the stroller.

"What could this be?" I said. Up ahead, a woman in a suit jacket tugged on the arm of a little boy who was being truculent, gesturing toward something.

This was the sort of mystery that occupied us pleasantly on our outings. You slumped in your chair and observed the passing lawns. The woman was full of energy, and not a pleasant sort. She yanked the boy fitfully toward a minivan.

"My doggy," wailed the child.

"Oh dear," I said to you. "That boy wants his doggy. His mommy isn't too happy about it."

She caught sight of us, advancing as innocuously as we could, and glared. That is, I took it to be a glare. Without my glasses, I am not capable of fine observation.

Perhaps the woman mistook me for your mother, one of those women who, past menopause, procreate with the help of modern technology. A woman in Italy gave birth to twins at the age of sixty-five, I believe, and there she was grinning from the newspaper with a face like a crumpled hanky and holding in her arms two infants who looked oddly like little old men. I am not even close to sixty-five yet. My hair is still brown.

I hoped the woman would see that I was your grandmother, and I thought to mention it, just to clarify things, but we passed the pair without an opportunity for disclosure. They hopped in the minivan and sped by us in the opposite direction.

"Oh dear," I said. "I do believe that is another loose dog."

This one was a young husky dragging a leash behind him as he hopped over a bush in a nearby lawn. He had gleaming, eerie blue eyes and appeared frisky. "Frisky is not what we're looking for," I said, turning on a dime and strolling back up the sidewalk.

We ducked down a side street. "Don't be concerned," I said. "If worse comes to worst, I can always grab his leash and pull him away from you."

You began crabbing a little bit. This was not unusual, I'd observed, and generally preceded nap time. It had nothing to do with the loose dog.

A minivan barrelled down our side street. "I could swear that's the same woman," I said. You could neither confirm nor deny this. The van swung recklessly around the corner. We seemed to be out of danger. Perhaps the husky had bored of his pursuit.

We were now hopelessly off course. The park seemed miles away, and my feet were growing weary. It had been unwise to wear a sandal with a heel on such an outing, but no one was around to prevent me from doing so.

"There's nothing like an old fool," I said.

We passed a schoolyard, deserted. The bell rang for recess, and within seconds, doors burst open and screaming children swarmed. You blinked but did not look at them. For you, the gentler observation, the drifting leaf, the late-flowering bush. The children's screams seemed an exaggeration of schoolyard joy. There was a distinct lack of adult supervision. I awaited the cry of misery, the sharp fall, the broken wrist, but a wall of protection, magical, surrounded their play.

"The park is this way," I said, although I could not be certain. "Just beyond those trees."

The minivan, the same one, I was sure, sped past us again. The husky sat in the back seat, looking princely. The child was no longer weeping. The woman offered a foul glance in our direction. "I'm not his mother," I wanted to explain, but her window was rolled up, and she was off now on other business.

I no longer had business to be off on. My days were open-ended. A cup of tea at an early hour, awake despite myself and staring from the window at the street-lit yards. Turn on the radio at low volume. Prepare a fruit crisp, but lack the appetite to eat it all myself. Who would? An entire fruit crisp. It goes soggy after a day on the counter or hard in the fridge, and then it's scrape, scrape, scrape into the garbage bin.

We reached the park, beyond those trees, just as I had hoped. It was fragrant and spacious and there was much shade in which to wander. The wheels of the stroller gnawed fitfully across the grass.

"Oh dear," I said, dread coming over me of a sudden. "The third dog." This was not a statement of fact. There was no third dog that we could see, not yet, but in my experience, there is always a third. Life unfolds randomly, and yet it has its patterns, observable, pointless, drab. My children would dispute this, with much groaning and rolling of the eyes, but it is true. Children will always groan at their parents' superstitions. It is no good to change your mind to suit them; you will never satisfy their instincts for separation.

Recently, I experienced the following: three strangely buzzing insects dying in my apartment. The first was a simple housefly, the second a small honeybee. But the third was iridescent, weirdly winged, and cross-legged, with a stinger like a toothpick. I pursued it to the window with a rolled-up newspaper, but it eluded me. I had never seen such an insect before, and my only thought was to swat it dead before it stung me to bits, but it flew across the room and vanished. I followed in my bedroom slippers and searched in vain. This was rather late at night, but I had been unable yet to sleep. It came to me then—three buzzing insects, a progression, a sign. My children would not have wanted to receive a late-night phone call on the subject, and I too could recognize its irrelevance, but I was afraid and felt I could not sleep. Where had the third insect gone?

I removed my slippers, sitting on the edge of the bed, and there it was, squashed on the bottom of one.

You sighed at this story, eyelids drooping, but you were not old enough yet to stand against me and state the case for coincidence. I could have brought up other examples in my defence, each of them as tiny and troubling as ripples on a flat pond—the day of the three mysterious hang-ups, the last one punctuated by heavy breathing; the day of the three squirrels dashing into traffic before my eyes, the last one getting crushed—but there was no need. You demanded nothing. Your skin was as clear as an egg when I bent to look. You were asleep.

I laid the stroller seat flat and continued through the park, alert for the third dog. It did not come.

~

All was quiet, too, on the park's perimeter, where stood a row of beautiful houses, each as individual and grand as a peacock feather. Glimpses into backyards like secret gardens revealed fall flowers, trellises, fish ponds, arbours. None of these were things I had been able to provide for your mother, or any of my children. We lived for their entire lives in one house, with a backyard as flat as a pancake, the grass burned to a crisp and a muddy vegetable garden in one corner. The garden appeared overgrown and rangy even in early spring, and I could never keep up with the tomatoes it produced, exhausted by pregnancy or late-night feedings or, later, a parade of duties that seemed never to slow or pass. Until one day they did, and I said to Frank, "Just when you think you'll never catch up, you do."

"I wish your mother could have had a secret garden," I said, as if this would have made all the difference.

You never knew what your children were lacking until you saw it played out in terrible parody later on, when as adults they stretched themselves around whatever had been missing, strangely misshapen. Your mother, for example. Your mother, furious over the most obscure slight, scouring all the cracks and crannies for proof that she wasn't loved as she ought to be. Now what did that mean? How did that child in braids, a languid girl swinging lazily from the jungle gym her father built, grow to a woman of such unhappy intent, all sharp chin and pointed fingers?

If we had given her a secret garden, with all the secrets intact and belonging to her, would she have needed to invent one for everyone else, over and over again? Such ugly gardens, too, of crabgrass and rotten vine. How I had hoped that with you in her arms, your mother would see for herself the truth of things, the helplessness of others.

I stopped to check that you were breathing. You were. Of course you were. It was from this angle, bent over your tiny frame, that I saw the gate swinging open on polished black hinges, inviting us to look closer.

"Oh dear," I said. "We're intruding." But I did not move.

Under a dark, weeping pine, a man with a hat held in his arms a woman of impressive proportions. Their embrace was profound, as if he were comforting her and she him, and if separated they would collapse. I stood rooted, ashamed but craving their intimacy, some small part of it. My chest ached. Longing; loss.

Frank always wore a hat. He looked smart in a hat. It wasn't the same hat over the years; he went through phases. At one point, he even favoured a knitted fisherman's cap. Never a beret, though. Too feminine.

If I had known in advance, would I have enjoyed all that passed before any whit less? Of course not. But perhaps I would have approached with caution such small offerings as a cup of coffee by the bedside, the brush of one arm against another accidentally in the kitchen, irritation erupting over shaving remains all over my bathroom sink; perhaps I would have drawn back, tried on something softer than demand.

I said nothing of this to you, and stopped myself from going further. Retrospect was a telescope turned the wrong way. It made disproportionate the rights and wrongs. It erased the moments in between.

We had paused for too long. The couple drew apart, and the woman ran her hand through the man's hat. The picture shifted. Something about it wasn't quite right. She caressed and scratched above the brim of his hat, which was not a hat after all. It was hair.

"Your mother will not believe this," I said to you, setting forth.

The man had turned his head in our direction, spying us. Babbling old lady pushing baby stroller. Foolish old woman rubbernecking, jowly as a turkey, goggle-eyed.

"Darn it, darn it, darn it," I said, and picked up the pace. I felt a creeping in my shoulder blades and glanced around to see whether we were being followed. The streets were so quiet, they felt deserted. The man with the hair hat stood on the sidewalk outside the gate, the jellyish woman nearby, watching our retreat. They began walking in the opposite direction, almost as rapidly as I had gone, as if they were intruders too.

"That garden gate was just open," I said to you. "Anyone could have come in or out."

How you slept, despite it all. You would sleep through the coming of the third dog too, or at least I hoped you would.

~

"Give me the baby!" said your mother, running to the back door to greet us.

"Shh, honey. He's asleep," I said, but your eyelids fluttered at the sound of her voice and you stirred.

"We saw a man who had hair like a hat," I told your mother, who was tugging at the straps that held you in place, grasping you under the armpits, pulling you into her chest. "He's still half asleep," I said.

"He misses his mommy," she said. "He wants some foodie."

"Well, shall I be off, then?"

"Did you say hair like a hat?"

"Oh, it was nothing. Just something we saw."

"You're always having adventures with your grandma, aren't you?" she said. You were coming awake like a man coming up from under water, blinking your eyes and gasping with a little fish mouth. Your mother kissed you on the cheek with fierce energy.

"Did you get done what you needed to?" I said.

"Hardly," she said. "The bastard."

"Oh, sweetheart," I said. "Maybe for the baby's sake . . ." But my voice trailed off. Don't put your oar in, Frank would have said. Or who knows what he would have said. He was a firm man when it came to the children. He would not tolerate their jumping on the bed or playing soccer in front of the house. He might have stuck his oar in, given the chance.

"Don't even start," your mother said, squeezing you against her viciously. "You don't know the half of it."

"I don't need to know," I said.

"No, you don't. You don't want to know."

"Well, shall I be off?"

"You could stay for lunch."

"Would you like me to?"

"Would I suggest it otherwise? Please."

I opened a can of tuna for us, spooned in mayonnaise and a dollop of relish. Your mother was nursing you, sunk into the sofa, head nodding over yours. She looked at you with love. I could see that from the kitchen. Was it my business to measure what sort of love, or how plentiful the pool? You gulped and sucked, so new to this planet and yet so clearly defined. You were what you were and what you would be rose up inside you, painting your features, your voice, your skin. I imagined that you would be a happy boy, jolly, adventurous, sprinting about the house on knobby legs.

But this would not necessarily be the case. I imagined your mother, when she was first born, to be a solemn child, lapping monkishly at my breast, but as a teenager she was wild, flying in and out of friendships, dating questionable boys with beat-up cars, brushing her face with soft blues and roses like bruises. So you did not know. You never knew until it arrived. This is why the imagination is so sweet, and so dangerous.

"Thanks, Mom," she said. "Just put the plate on the coffee table. I'll eat in a minute."

"Is everything okay?" I said.

"Pardon?" she said, lifting her long, sad face to me.

"Is everything all right? Can I do anything for you?"

"It'll be fine."

"Is there a chance," I said, "for reconciliation?"

"That's not the point," she said. "You wouldn't forgive him either, if you knew."

I squeezed my hands together, ring catching skin, and thought, Wouldn't I?

I assumed, as most might, that there was some affair in the works, perhaps ended or perhaps ongoing. These things happen, I wanted to say to your mother. Such is life. Forgive and forget. But there were things she would not want to know either, secrets best left boxed and under the bed. We were lucky ones, Frank and I. We found ways to go on, and reasons to hold each other late at night, and even in broad daylight.

My daughter, I would say, if only I were brave enough, if only my throat would allow it. My daughter, to marry is to be hurt in one way or another. So be it. To marry is to cleave to another.

The phone rang. Your mother sat stock still, nursing you, like a statue of Madonna and child.

"Shall I get that?"

"Don't."

"I'll go, I think," I said, hesitating.

"Thanks for making me lunch," she said, although the sandwich remained untouched.

When I bent to kiss her on the cheek, she did not flinch.

Outside the sun beat upon me, and I searched up and down the pavement for the third dog. There was a bark from the neighbouring lawn, behind the hedge. But the dog was tied up. It was not the third dog. I walked slowly along the side-walk to the bus stop. A stream of traffic lilted past.

Frank, I said to myself. Frank, our daughter is an unhappy woman. You might even say that she is a miserable woman, I said, and I mean that in every sense of the word.

My apartment, new in the past five years, awaited me. I sold the house where the children grew up, and they all said, How wonderful. Won't it be lovely to live in a brand-new place? As if "brand new" were synonymous with "good." They were of a generation that believed happiness could be purchased, uncreased and fresh and newly minted. You will not be of this generation. You will find your own route to happiness. For me, happy were those walls marked with pen, where the children stood to be measured; happy was the spotty yard out back; happy was your grandfather's ghost knocking on the door to what had once been our bedroom and was now just mine. The children would not have it. I made the mistake of saying the word "ghost" in their presence, and that was that.

"Do you need a transfer?" said the bus driver, a plump woman with a comely hairdo.

"No," I said. "It's not far to my apartment."

The bus swayed, and I scurried to find an empty seat. There was a German shepherd on board with a blind man, but this was not the third dog.

Frank, I said, looking out the window and reminding myself that I was not so very old, that I should really forgo this habit of talking to myself. Frank, I said. Have I missed the third dog?

I was afraid, you see, that I would see it everywhere.

I knew enough to mention such foolishness to no one but Frank, and you. You were yet so young. You could take nothing from me; you were resilient, untouchable. That, my dear, was a relief. Enough harm done already.

Don't pity yourself, I said. Now is not the time.

That's right, said Frank. The third dog may not come. Just this once.

MISSING

"WOULD YOU LIKE to ring the doorbell?" I said to Thomson. Over one shoulder, I had a diaper bag, purchased before the baby's arrival and therefore too small, too sleek, too optimistic for its purposes. Thomson climbed out of the stroller and handed his sun hat to me.

"Thank you," I said. "Thank you, but this belongs on your head."

The stroller folded like a striped umbrella, and I leaned it against the pale yellow brick wall.

"I'll lift you up, and you ring the doorbell," I said. "Not that one. This one." I was sweating under the arms and certain to be red in the face, unadorned, overwrought. There had been the long, hot drive down the 401, finding parking at the farthest subway stop, riding the train downtown, with Thomson temporarily placated by Cheerios and changing scenery. It had not been an easy venture. I had planned it meticulously, each step listed in order on paper ripped from a notepad, overseen by my husband.

My mother on the phone this morning: "Would you like me to come along? Or watch Thomson for the day? You know I'd love to."

"No, no. We'll be fine."

"Call as soon as you get home or I'll worry."

My husband kissing me half awake before he left for work: "I filled the car with gas for you."

Thomson poked at the buzzer. It would have sounded in fits and jolts at its destination. "That's good," I said, stopping his hand in my own.

The intercom crackled. "Who's there?" It was the second time I'd heard his voice, a blurry, grizzled voice that could have belonged to a hard drinker, or, then again, to someone with a cold in his head.

There on the stoop, with the list balled up in the diaper bag, I was not as brave as the sum of my actions. Thomson eyed me curiously.

"Who's there? Hello?"

The greeting echoed forlornly, and I clutched Thomson against my neck. The list, I thought, the list. As if the weight of all that came before pressed against the final step, printed out in neat letters, the way in labour you have no choice but to push. "It's me. Sylvia," I said.

"Sylvia. Come in, please."

There were two flights of narrow stairs to climb, the stroller under one arm, the diaper bag over the other, Thomson somewhere in between. "Hold on to my neck," I said. The steps under my slapping Birkenstocks were covered in brown-and-white linoleum, so you could not tell whether they were clean or dirty, but there was a faint whiff of urine rising in the heat. The hallway was yellowing, humming with three low-watt bulbs.

"This is it," I said. He must have been waiting for us, peering out from the peephole, because the door opened with a flourish, natural light streaming out.

"Welcome," said my grandfather, reaching for the stroller. "You poor thing. So hot, so much to carry."

I had been expecting any number of vague and shapeless things for all of my twenty-six years, and in an instant, they solidified into one man wearing a brisk Hawaiian-patterned shirt and khaki shorts and a hat. But it was not a hat, because it was growing from his scalp. I was reminded of those several days postpartum, when the newness of responsibility crashed up against all those hormones, and I wept in fear over Thomson's tiny, fragile head, thinking, I cannot do this.

"Did you have any trouble finding the place?"

"No," I said, and tried to smile.

"You will be wondering about this." He touched his hair.

"Oh. No, no."

"I did it after she disappeared. I wanted to do something different, to feel different."

"I see."

"Every time I go to cut it off now, I can't."

"A hat," I said.

"A hat," he said.

A kettle rattled on the stove, broke into a fierce whistle. He did not seem to notice, shaking his head and smiling at us. "And this is your little boy."

"Thomson," I said, shouting over the kettle. "We thought we'd call him Tom or Tommy, but he's ended up Thomson."

"Come in," he said. "Sylvia. Come in, Thomson."

We were standing in the doorway, halfway in and halfway out. "The kettle," I said helplessly. It was making me frantic.

"You will excuse me." In retreat, his hair looked exactly like a hat.

“Come along,” I said to Thomson, stepping fully into the apartment. I placed him on the floor, which was comforting, well-swept and worn grey vinyl tiles. My grandfather had leaned the stroller against the wall, and there it stood, also comforting. The light in the place was golden and green, despite the tipsy walls and stooped ceiling. Be careful, I thought. Be kind. I smoothed the sundress, billowy and bright, over my belly.

The door to the yellowing hallway was still open, our escape route. Close it, I thought. It seemed an act of goodwill almost beyond me, just out of reach, a step on the list I had not foreseen. I put my hand on the porcelain doorknob and pushed. Click. We were in. We were trapped. We were home.

“Follow me,” said my grandfather from a doorway opposite, a shadow against the light streaming in. “Welcome.” He spread his hands to the grey tabletop, on which rested a pot of honey and a sugar bowl. “I did not know which you preferred in your tea.”

“Thank you. Sugar is fine.” A breeze played through the kitchen window behind my back, cooling the strands of hair sticking to my neck. “This is a lovely space.”

We sat on metal chairs with plastic puffy seats to which my thighs were already sticking. The windowsill was lined with plants: ivies and ferns and a strange flowering shrub of rioting pink. Thomson yanked open a cupboard door and discovered pots and pans.

"Don't worry," said my grandfather. "No harm in that."

I sipped the cup of tea and ate a chocolate-covered biscuit, the chocolate sticking to my fingertips. This was my parallel life.

"You are expecting another?" he said.

"In November," I said. At the sound of my voice, or the spike of chocolate, the baby punched in my belly. "We don't know what Thomson will make of it. Being a big brother."

Thomson heard his name and turned, opening his mouth. I popped a piece of biscuit on his tongue.

"You have brothers and sisters?" said my grandfather.

"One brother. He's quite a bit younger."

"We just had the one. Just Leigh-Ann."

In the centre of the table, between us, was a photograph on which my sight kept snagging. From this angle, it looked like a woman and a man, a young woman with feathered hair and a wide smile beside an older man.

"Yes," he said. "That's her. There aren't many pictures of us together." He drew the photograph to him and looked into it like the figures there might animate themselves. "She was many things, you know. Not always so happy."

Thomson banged a lid against a pot, his mouth turning bird-like to me again. "More cookie?" I said.

"You will want to see her." My grandfather's lips moved gently behind the crashing of pot and lid. He slid the photograph along the table, and there she was.

"I don't look like her," I said. There was a brief pause in Thomson's hammering, and my words flew into and out of it.

"Maybe the eyes," said my grandfather.

Her face should have belonged to me. I had expected it would, and it did not. It was particular in its lines, some of them hardened where in a young woman they should have been soft; and in its colours, bleached strands of hair, small green eyes, frosted pink lipstick; and in its expression, which was happy, split with joy.

"I can see her in your gestures," said my grandfather. "I'm not sure how."

I did not think this possible. I had barely moved since our arrival, barely lifted a hand to brush away hair or fiddled with a teacup or made any extraneous motion.

"Ma," said Thomson. "Mamama." I dropped another fragment onto his tongue.

"Like that," said my grandfather.

"Pardon?"

"The way you give him the cookie."

"Who did she give cookies to?" I said; I knew it was not me.

"I don't know," he said. "I didn't mean that in particular; it just reminded me somehow."

I watched the photograph, waiting for stillness to resolve into truth.

"She was very young, you know, not quite sixteen. Then she never seemed to grow up. She disappeared in 1986."

In 1986, I attended the sixth grade at Centennial Public School in Waterloo, Ontario. I had a favourite purple outfit: lavender pants, frilly purple shirt, and sateen purple underwear. I was not popular, but I was not hated. The girl who was hated had to see a psychiatrist weekly. She got out of class early to go. I remember her better than anyone else: her big bug eyes behind round glasses, her peculiar, old-fashioned clothes. Once, I offered to give her my old bike. I thought she didn't have a bike because she was poor. But she wasn't poor. She just did not like to ride her bike. She sneered at my old bike.

The thing linking us, the thread of pity, was that we were both adopted.

I never had to see a psychiatrist. I did not know what the difference was, but I held it against me like a shield, and I was never in danger, not of that kind.

"What are your parents like?" said my grandfather.

"They're lovely," I said. "I don't know how to describe them."

"Were you hoping?" he said, and looked at the photograph in my hand.

"I didn't want a new mother. I just wanted to know."

Thomson stood and toddled to my leg. I rummaged in the diaper bag for his sippy cup of juice.

"I was thinking," said my grandfather. "I wish I had a story to give you."

"Oh."

"I'm not much good at stories."

"You don't need to feel . . ." I said, stroking Thomson's soft round head. His eyes were slightly glazed. It was approaching nap time.

"We should go into the sitting room," said my grandfather. "Your boy could lie on the sofa."

"Thank you," I said. "We are both a little tired." I could not release the photograph, although I had not looked into it for several minutes.

"This way." My grandfather inclined his head, and I knew he understood about the photograph. He had not wanted to let it go either.

A metal fan with a revolving head perched in a corner of the small room and the blinds were drawn. "Rest here," said my grandfather, leaning over and patting a velour sofa patterned with hummingbirds in turquoise, pink, beige. Thomson lay with his head in my rounded lap, eyelids fluttering. The photograph rested in my fingers beside my thigh. Out of the corner of my eye, I saw the laughing girl, her exposed throat.

My grandfather drew up a metal TV table and placed my cup of tea upon it, within reach. From the ceremony of our new arrangement, I expected something momentous: perhaps a clicking film projector with footage of my mother at an early birthday party, running into the water at the beach, opening Christmas presents under a sparkling tree.

My grandfather sat in a lumpy rocker beneath a ragged spider fern and rubbed his brow. "I've been thinking and thinking of what I could tell you."

I nodded.

"When she went missing, we didn't realize it for two months. Two months. She never called home much. By the time we figured something was wrong, it was too late. We were divorced by then," he said. "We took a plane out to Vancouver, where she'd been staying, and walked all up and down the streets with her picture. 'Have you seen this girl, our daughter? Her name is Leigh-Ann.'"

He waited. In his mind were pictures I could not see. I imagined this man, a younger version of himself with ordinary hair, walking wet streets with his estranged wife. The pair of them turned into each other for this flat, grey moment in time. Stopping the women, the picture of their girl in the palm of his hand, or hers. Surrounding them, bearing in on their search, were chain-link fences, garbage pooled against flooded grates, empty lots, and boarded doorways. Have you seen this girl, our daughter?

This may have been true, or not. I had never been to Vancouver. I did not know what my grandfather saw there, or how many days he searched before the word "missing" overwhelmed everything else his daughter had been.

"People had seen her," said my grandfather. "But not for a while."

We had settled in now. I did not need to reply.

"I tried to think of a happy story."

"That's okay," I said.

"I don't know if she got to hold you after you were born. She never said. I never asked. We were just glad to have her home again."

"It's okay."

"We kept the clothes she left behind in her room, and the makeup. That was all. You don't want those, do you?"

"No," I said. The thought of picking through a cardboard box layered with her jeans and blouses, her mascara and rouge, sent sickness into my throat like a giant empty belch.

When I mentioned, after my wedding, that I was thinking of looking for my birth mother, my own mother said, "Go with God." We were standing in the lobby of the reception hall with nearly everyone gone home. My feet were bare. I had expected all evening that I would at some point begin to weep, but there was nothing in me save laughter. I was filled to the brim with joy.

"You are beautiful," said my mother. "I'm so proud."

"I was thinking," I said. The words I had been carrying for so long spilled over, uncontained, just as I felt. "I was thinking . . . Who was she?"

"You want to know," my mother said, as if she'd been waiting all her life for me to say this.

"I don't need another mother," I said.

"Of course you don't," she said. We embraced so rarely that our arms scarcely knew what to do with the body opposite. She was all ribs and elbows under crackling beige chiffon. "Go with God." She meant it as a blessing on my hopes and fears, but the words came back to me in my grandfather's living room, wrung with warning. This other life flowered in front of my face, went from blossom to burst bloom in an instant.

"I have never been a grandfather," said my grandfather. "I am probably getting it all wrong."

"No, no," I said. Thomson sighed under my hand, his cheek serene and emptied of care. In my other hand, the photograph waited. I opened my fingertips and let it slide onto the velour, away from me.

“He’s a beautiful baby,” said my grandfather.

“Sometimes I can’t believe he’s mine.”

“That’s what we said about Leigh-Ann.”

“I thought I would look like her. That’s what I imagined.”

He nodded and would not look at me; instead, his eyes slipped to the escaped photograph. The fan’s breath swept over us.

What I imagined had taken so many faces, so many guises. It changed shape like a travelling carnival descending on a grassy farmer’s field, the bodies spun into action, the tents thrown over this and that, the shouts of the people watching and waiting. In 1986, I imagined my mother in the gentle pear shape of my French teacher, Madame Russell, her blond hair falling around her shoulders like a cloud. In 1996, I imagined her tracking me down, secretly attending my graduation from university. She was in the rows of faces as I strode across the podium in flowing robes, anxious about tripping in my brand-new high heels. In 1998, I wished her into my wedding, not front and centre but a blur, a shadow in the background of the posed photographs, a face caught and trapped, willingly.

She did not lie in front of my eyes or block my vision, but she was here and there, darting and skittering across the floor of my thoughts, always an invention on the cusp of discovery.

"Will he sleep long?" said my grandfather.

"Probably not. Just a catnap."

The details were not here. In my heart, I knew they never had been.

"I would like to give you something," said my grandfather. He stood and wandered the room, touching delicate china trinkets that did not look like they belonged to him. There was a shepherdess with a crook, a brown-and-white spaniel, a girl in a green dress, a boy with a fishing pole, a cottage with a thatched roof, two children leaning elbows on a railing over a brown bridge.

"We gave these to her as birthday gifts. Not my idea."

"They're sweet."

"I can't remember which birthday was which thing."

"It doesn't matter."

He held the girl in the green dress in the palm of his hand. She had brown, formed hair and an insipid painted face. In her hands was a clutch of violets. "Would you like this one?"

"Please, don't feel like—"

"I want to give you something. This is my favourite."

"It's beautiful."

"It doesn't look a thing like her. She didn't wear dresses."

"It's beautiful."

"Let me wrap it up for you."

He returned with a bulky oblong wrapped in grocery bags, which I squeezed into the diaper bag. Thomson stirred and cried as I leaned forward. He often cried when he first woke up. I stroked his hot skin and pulled him into my armpit. The photograph slid down between the cushions. We watched it get eaten up.

"She was a bit wild," said my grandfather. "But I've always maintained that she had a good heart."

I stood.

"I wanted to tell you a good story about her."

I reached for the diaper bag. Thomson wriggled into my skin.

"She had lots of friends. They were in and out of the house like a pack of butterflies."

"Thank you for the tea," I said. "And the cookies." We were walking to the front door.

"She pored over those fashion magazines. She always had the latest hairstyle." My grandfather picked up the stroller as I touched the porcelain doorknob. We slipped into the yellowing hallway.

"I remember she found a baby bird on the sidewalk and brought him home. I made him a bed in a shoebox. She cried all alone in her room when he died. 'Go away,' she said."

The linoleum snapped beneath our feet, and we were suddenly back out into sunshine. I stood on the concrete stoop, dazed. My grandfather clasped the stroller between his elbows and fiddled with it.

"Pull that part," I said. "It opens like an umbrella."

"The things they can do these days," he said.

I placed Thomson in the open stroller and strapped him in. "Thank you," I said.

"You should visit again. Bring your husband."

"Yes. I will."

"She never meant any harm. I've always said that."

"I believe you."

"Do you?" he said, and reached for my hand.

"Of course," I said.

I had grown used to his hair hat. It looked, for this moment, plausible. I should have brought along a camera. I should have asked a passerby to take a photograph of the three of us. Next time, I thought. But next time is so rare. It's a hummingbird in the rose bushes: blink and its possibility is gone.

"Goodbye, little man," said my grandfather, his knees cracking as he bent in front of Thomson, who stretched his hands out and grabbed the hair shaped like a hat.

"Thomson!" I said sharply.

"Isn't that something," said my grandfather, laughing. "He's a strong little fellow."

"I'm sorry," I said, reaching for Thomson's hands, my

own brushing the hair too. It felt softer than I'd expected, like moss.

"I don't mind at all." My grandfather stood up, gentlemanly and raffish. Loose strands poked out at odd places where Thomson had been, but the basic shape was unchanged. "He's just being himself," said my grandfather. "More people should be themselves; the world would be a different place."

"Goodbye, then," I said, lifting my hand and letting it fall. I could feel his hair against it still: foreign. We did not embrace. We did not seem to know how.

"Goodbye, my dear."

~

People parted like the sea as I pushed the stroller along the sidewalk. No one looked into my face. I licked wet salt from the edge of my lip. "Spare change," said not one man but three, and a girl who sat inside a sleeping bag despite the heat.

"I'm so sorry," I said. No one else said anything.

The steps to the trains were slick like bathroom tile. Thomson sat as still as a bird as I dragged the stroller backwards down them. As the train rattled into the station, stale air sweeping the skirt of my dress up, Thomson breathed inward, a deep gasp.

"Ah," I said, sliding onto the plastic bench. Thomson climbed out of his stroller and into my lap, wrapping his fingers in my hair. This was a favourite game. "Careful of Mommy's tummy," I said, but he only wanted to get closer, to be as near as possible. This is the luxury of babies.

"He's a pretty boy," said the woman sitting next to us. She poked in the air at Thomson. "Pretty boy, pretty boy. Why doesn't he smile? Where's his teeth?"

"He's only got two teeth so far. He's a late teether," I said. Thomson would not look at her.

"These are my real teeth," she said, drawing her lips back, grinning. "I'm an actress."

"Oh," I said.

"I'm on my way to audition for a toothpaste commercial." She grinned again, wildly, so that her gums showed.

"Yes," I said.

"My agent thinks they'll like me. He thinks I'm perfect." Her back was rounded into a steep hump, skin pasty and wizened, thin grey hair barely covering the front of her scalp. But her teeth were magnificent: white, pearled, spilling from her mouth. Who knew? The story could be true. It was unlikely to be true, but it could be true.

"I need to get off at Ossington station. Can you tell me when that is?"

"Certainly."

"You're a sweet girl, a good girl."

She did not speak again, just turned every few minutes to show me her teeth and nod her head. I nodded in return, encouragingly, I hoped.

"It's not this stop; it's the next stop," I said. And then, "This is your stop."

"Oh, thank you, thank you. It's for Colgate. Look for me."

"I will."

~

The china figure came out of the plastic bags intact. Something in me had expected mutilation. I set it on the kitchen counter, then moved it around the house from shelf to shelf, to the TV cabinet, and finally to the upstairs bathroom, where it sat on top of the mirrored cupboard.

"She looks like you," said my husband.

It was the sort of thing he was likely to say; maybe it was the reason I had married him, intimating in advance the kindnesses he could offer, their ordinary flights, their keen necessity.

I looked for the woman in the Colgate commercial. I was patient, but she did not appear. My husband thought perhaps she had been a crazy, but I did not believe it. Two years went by. Then one morning, I was flipping through channels to find the Teletubbies, and there she was. Her smile was enormous. She winked at me.

When we see the missing, at last, do we turn in the opposite direction, or do we stand and wait, stand and wait, stand and wait.

CHOSEN

"THERE ARE BUBBLES EVERYWHERE. Just do it," said Lucy, puffing over my shoulder.

"But how?" I said.

"Just take the spatula, and—" She reached to grab it.

"Okay," I said, poking at the pancake. "Okay." It lumped over halfway and stuck onto itself.

"The inside won't cook that way," said Lucy. "That's not how you do it."

"You do it, then," I said. "I hate cooking."

"You do not hate cooking," said Mrs. Shantz, overhearing as she marched around the classroom. "You just need practice. Let her try again, Lucy."

I flipped the other pancake perfectly, but the underside was burnt black.

"Well done," said Mrs. Shantz. "Just a little earlier next time."

"My turn," said Lucy, scooping blueberry batter onto the flat, hot pan. "See? You wait until it bubbles, then you just know, then you flip it."

Ryan poked me in the arm with his pencil.

"Don't," I said. I checked my sleeve for a mark.

"So are you going to the dance?" he said.

"I don't know." Grade seven was the first year for dances after school. I skipped the one in the fall. Lucy skipped too. Dancing wasn't for us. The sort of girl it was for was Molly Edgerton, who had long flat hair and pink bubblegum lip gloss. She wore a push-up padded bra with lace. We had seen it while changing for gym.

Lucy had a bra that her older sister did not want any more, grey in the straps. She was big, but it was mostly fat. Some days she liked being big, other days she hated it. Boys noticed. Boys had pulled her bra strap. Personally, I thought she was lying when she said she hated it.

I had a training bra that my mother picked out for me at Eaton's. She dragged me along. She said I had buds on my chest and I needed a bra. The way she said "buds" made the whole thing sound disgusting.

"Leigh-Ann, get your buns over here and try this on," she called, but I stood quietly in the socks section and pretended I did not know who she was. "She's at that age," I heard her tell the saleslady.

The training bra did not even fit. It was too big. How sad was that—a training bra that was too big. It looked puckered under my shirts. "If you'd only tried it on at the store," said my mother. "They don't care. Nobody cares."

I noticed I wasn't wearing the bra today. "I don't know," I said about the dance.

"Are you scared to go?" said Ryan.

"No," I said.

"Then why don't you go."

"I don't know," I said.

Lucy flipped two pancakes onto a plate. They looked delicious. They were round and just brown with blueberries melting in them.

"Everybody takes a turn," sang Mrs. Shantz, clapping her hands. "Boys too."

Ryan yanked on my apron string.

"Stop it," I said, reaching back, and he grabbed my hand. "Let go."

"Everyone has to participate," called Mrs. Shantz. "Just five more minutes till cleanup."

"You guys have to do it," said Lucy, pointing the spatula at Ryan and Jason. "I'm not getting a crummy mark just because of you."

"Do you want me to do it?" said Ryan to me.

"I don't care," I said. He had dropped my hand.

"I'll do it," said Jason.

"No, I will," said Ryan.

"You both have to. Someone just do it."

"If Leigh-Ann goes to the dance, I will," said Ryan.

"Don't be a moron," said Lucy. "You have to do it anyway."

"Maybe I'll go," I said. And then to Lucy: "Maybe we should go."

"You're the one who never wants to go," said Lucy. "I'll go."

"Well, I'll go if you go."

Ryan grabbed the spatula and pretended to whack me on the bottom.

"Three more minutes," shouted Mrs. Shantz. The room was giddy and hot with noise. We were all sick of wearing aprons.

Jason dumped the rest of the batter in the pan, one giant pancake flowing to the sides and spilling over onto the burner. It spattered and smoked and smelled like supper at our house. Mom was always leaving things on the stove and going off to do something else. To cool them, she threw the pots out onto the balcony, where they melted circles in the snow, the food inside stuck to the bottom. Toasted cheese sandwiches again.

"Moron," said Lucy. "You have to clean that up, you know."

"When do I flip it?" said Ryan to Lucy. He was just teasing. "When do I flip it the bird?"

"You don't even know what that means," said Lucy. I did not know what it meant.

"Two more minutes, then cleanup. Get moving, folks."

Ryan was pudgy, with rolls of fat under his T-shirt like a small pile of bicycle inner tubes. His face was sweaty, and his hand too. "Flip it the birdie, flip it the bird," he said, sticking the spatula into the middle of the pancake to test whether it was done.

"You've wrecked it," said Lucy. "Who wants to eat that?"

"A for effort," said Mrs. Shantz when Lucy had washed the pan and bowl and I'd scrubbed the burner. "Everybody tried." We were allowed to eat the pancakes with syrup. Lucy shared one of hers with me.

"I can't wear this to the dance," I whispered to Lucy. I was wearing regular pants. I didn't tell her, but I also did not have ten cents to pay for admission. "There isn't time to go home," I said.

"So call your mom," said Lucy. Everyone was pushing outside homeroom.

"Single file," yelled Mrs. Maloney, our homeroom teacher. She was waiting for silence before we went in. Ryan's name for her was Mrs. Baloney.

Lucy wore a short jean skirt, not quite a mini. Her round legs were covered in violet fuzzy tights. She always had money, for snacks or gum.

"She won't be home," I said.

"Call your dad—he's always home. Go to the office now and call."

"May I be excused?" I raised my hand.

"Where are you off to?" said Mrs. Maloney.

"I need to go to the office."

"Don't whisper. I can't hear you."

"I need to go to the office."

"She's got her pe-ri-od," sang Ryan. My face turned a terrible red, hot creeping up from my neck into my hair. I had never got my period, not even once. I was waiting for it, but it wasn't my time yet. "Your time will come," my mother said, after mentioning the buds again.

"Go ahead," said Mrs. Baloney. I called her that in my head.

~

Dad was waiting for me after school. He had walked from home. I told him to stay at the end of the school driveway, but instead he was hanging around the front doors, holding a brown grocery bag with the top folded down. I grabbed the bag.

"Don't you want to check and see that I brought everything okay?" he said. He was smoking a cigarette. His hands were cold and red with no gloves on, even though the ground was covered in snow. "I wasn't sure about which skirt."

"It's okay," I hissed and waved my hands at him to stop talking, to go away. I ran into the school, the bag knocking against my leg.

"Is your dad still standing out there?" said Lucy, looking down the hallway with the lockers banging open and shut.

"No," I said, crossing my fingers behind my back that it wasn't him.

"I think he is."

"Oh," I said.

"He's waving."

"Don't look at him."

"I think he wants something."

"Oh God," I said, trudging to the doors as streams of students swarmed and shouted. Everyone would know he was my dad.

"You forgot your money for the dance," he said, tossing his cigarette butt on the patch of cleared-off concrete and reaching in his pants pocket. His jeans were too tight. His legs looked like sticks. He looked like a stick-man. I had never noticed before. He put the dime into my hand.

"Have fun, butterfly," he said and tried to give me a hug. I didn't move my arms or turn my head. "Okay, honey. Have fun."

I did not say goodbye. I did not look at him or see him walk away down the big hill, skidding in the snow in his grey running shoes, trying to squeeze his hands into his pockets.

I forgot him.

"I'm going in," said Lucy. There was already a line outside the gymnasium. Two teachers stood at the open metal doors taking money and ripping off tickets. It was dark behind them, with checkers of light thrown from a silver ball overhead. You could hear music, something fast for fast dancing. Three girls from our class waved to us.

"Wait for me," I said. "I have to get changed."

"We'll just be in there," Lucy said, and she floated away to join the girls.

~

There were grade eights passing around lipstick in front of the washroom mirrors.

"I like this colour."

"It's called Shocking Pink."

"It's so pretty on you."

"Do you think?"

"My mother would kill me if she saw."

The paper bag rustled when I opened it in the stall. It was the right skirt—the one I had thought I wanted—but I saw now that it was all wrong: a baby skirt, frilly, down to the ankles and off-white. It glowed. I looked like a glowing puffball.

The floor was cold under my socks. I had not thought to ask for different shoes.

I sat on the toilet. I would have to wear my winter boots. I would have to wear the skirt. What else could I do?

It will be fine, I whispered to myself. It's dark in there anyway.

The grade eights were brushing and spritzing their hair with sickening sweet spray. I bent forward to push into the boots and caught another smell, not good, sour and bitter and hot. I sniffed again. Oh no. Oh God, please, no. The smell was coming from me, from the pits of my arms.

My heart crashed into my stomach. That's me that stinks.

I could never leave the bathroom now. I would be trapped here forever in the glowing skirt and stinking sweater—ordinarily my favourite, hot pink with geometric shapes splashed across it. It would never again be my favourite. My mother would demand to know why I never wore it any more.

The girls from grade eight left, voices echoing off the walls and falling into silence.

I was alone.

I picked up the paper bag. It all seemed hopeless. It all seemed hopeless, but I could not stay here for the rest of my life. At the sinks, I scrubbed my armpits with paper towel. The sweater got wet. The girl in the mirror looked back at me, a plain face, a little girl's face. The back of my hair stood up in a cowlick. I wished that I was grown up, then I would know exactly what to do. Then I could do whatever I wanted.

The halls were deserted, except for the distant thump of music shaking the polished floors. "You have to go," I said. "You have to."

"Who are you talking to?" Ryan put his head up, water running down his chin. I had not seen him leaning over the drinking fountain.

"Nobody." I did not know whether to close my locker. I kept one hand on the paper bag.

"You said you were going to the dance."

"I am."

"Then why aren't you at the dance."

"Why aren't you."

"Just getting a drink." Ryan's T-shirt hung too large in the front, stretched out thin.

"I'm going now," I said.

"So go."

"I am." I jammed the locker shut with my knee. I wished that he would stop looking at me. I could hardly move with him watching like that. It felt as if I could not lift my feet properly or swing my arms, as if I had forgotten how. I knew I would stumble. I knew he would laugh at the salt stains on my boots.

At the doors, I handed over the dime. Ryan did the same.

"I thought you were already at the dance," I said.

"I was waiting for someone," he said.

"Finally!" shouted Lucy, running over in the dark. "What took you so long?" She was frantic with happiness. "We've been dancing and dancing. I'm so hot. I need a break."

We stood against the polished concrete wall with some other girls. My eyes were adjusting. The crowd thinned out for a slow dance. In the middle, under the silver ball, Molly Edgerton was glued to John Beemer, swaying against him. They barely shuffled their feet. His arms wrapped all the way around her, almost touching her bottom.

"They've been slow dancing every dance, even the fast ones," whispered Lucy. "It's disgusting."

John Beemer was the boy we both liked. But, then, so did everyone. He was slender, with blond shaggy hair and dark eyes, and he was mean. He could be nice and say hello and then the next day walk by like you were invisible, or worse. Like you were a nothing, a zero, a loser.

"Do you want to dance with Peter?" said a boy standing in front of me. I did not know who he was talking to. "Leigh-Ann," he said, "Peter wants to know if you want to dance."

"The song is almost over," I said. I did not want to dance with Peter. He was shorter than me and wore the same pants every day.

"The next song?" said the boy.

"No," I said.

The boy walked across the gym to Peter, who was standing with another boy, all of them all wrong. They huddled together and looked sad, although it was hard to see in the dark.

"I can't believe he asked you," said Lucy.

"I know," I said.

The boy pushed back toward us. Lucy groaned. "Will you dance with P.J.?"

"No."

"Will you dance with me?"

"No." I pretended he wasn't standing in front of me. I hoped no one would see us talking. It was just my luck, it was just my fate, to be asked to dance by the worst of the losers.

That's when I felt a space where Lucy should have been. I turned to see her following a boy from grade eight onto the dance floor. He pulled her hand, and she followed like a puppy dog, smiling back at us helplessly. She draped her arms over his shoulders and leaned into his chest as if she had been at a million dances and had done this a million times. He was taller than her.

The girls from our class were whispering, and I could not hear what they were saying. I was standing right beside them, but they leaned away from me.

"So you won't dance with any of us?" said the boy, who was still there.

"No," I said angrily, watching Lucy. The boy from grade eight breathed into her hair.

"We didn't want to anyway. It was just a dare. Ryan dared us."

I was going to slip out quietly and go to the washroom. I was going to slip out quietly and sit on the toilet in a stall, and I was not going to cry. Lucy would never know. As my dad would say, worse things could happen. Worse things have.

"Leigh-Ann," said Ryan, standing in my way.

"What," I said.

"Do you want to dance?"

"What?" I said.

"I said, do you want to dance?"

"With you?" I said. If I was brave, I would have said, "Get out of here. Who do you think you are, telling losers to dance with me?" I would have said, "Get out of my face." Mom said that two nights ago to Dad, then she cried and he put his arms around her, and he said, "I know you didn't mean that. I know you didn't." And she said, "Why do I say these things? What is wrong with me?" Nothing is wrong. Nothing.

"What's the matter? Are you scared to dance?"

I was not brave. I looked past him to where Lucy was

holding on to the guy from grade eight. They were waiting for the next song to start.

"Okay," I said. Maybe it wasn't John Beemer. Maybe it wasn't a guy from grade eight. At least it wasn't the worst of the losers.

I had never put my hands on a boy on purpose. His shoulders were squishy and damp. I had to bend at the elbows to keep my armpits clamped shut. Please, please, please, do not let him smell me, I whispered to myself.

His hands shook on my waist, just above the hip bones. We could not seem to get any closer than this, nothing touching. I did not know where to put my feet. They were between his, and he kept stepping on my boot.

"I'm sorry," he said, kicking my toes.

"That's okay," I said.

I did not care that he was pudgy and sweating. He was okay to hold on to. He was okay.

Over his shoulder, I saw the guy from grade eight kiss Lucy on the neck, sucking the skin. She had her eyes closed. She did not see me.

"Thanks," I said, when the song ended. Our hands dropped to our sides.

"Give your boyfriend a kiss," shouted Peter, running at us. He pushed, and Ryan's head smashed against my boob, one of the buds. It hurt horribly, a deep, sharp ache. I had to stop myself from covering the pain with my hand. But worse was knowing that his head had touched me there, his cheek. I could not look at him.

"Loser," said Ryan. "Fucking loser."

Lucy rushed over. "What happened?" she said. "I didn't really see. I just heard that guy, and then I saw you."

"Nothing," I said.

"So," said Lucy significantly, looking at Ryan, who was storming after Peter. "So? Are you guys, like . . ."

"It was just one dance."

"He's okay," said Lucy. "He's funny some of the time."

"I guess," I said.

"I have to go now. It's almost the last dance." The guy from grade eight was standing behind her, waiting. He was in charge of her now. She smiled and shrugged, like she had no choice. "I'll call you later," she whispered. She did not want to have a choice.

Peter got a bloody nose. He was out in the hall with a bloody nose, crying and snuffling. A teacher pressed wet paper towel on his face. I hurried to my locker for the bag, hoping they would not see me, trying to stay invisible. I could not wait to take off the puffy skirt.

When I came out of the washroom, Ryan was waiting for me. He ducked out from the indent of a classroom door, where he had been hiding.

"They're going to get me," he said. "I'll be suspended."

"Oh," I said. I did not know what else to say.

"You should care," he said. "I did it for you."

"Oh," I said, again. I did not know whether I should thank him. I did not know the right thing to say.

"Let's go out this way," he said, pointing to a side door, grabbing me by the arm. He seemed to assume that we would leave together. "No one will see."

"I need to get my coat."

"I'll wait here." He shivered. His coat was brown and worn through at the elbows.

You know, I could have gone to my locker and left by the front doors. I almost did. But as I slammed the locker door shut, I looked up and saw Lucy bursting out of the gym with the guy from grade eight, his arm tenderly over her shoulder, casually and tenderly, as if golden light were falling on them, her face turned to his. And I did not.

"Where do you live?" said Ryan. We pushed out the side door and it was already dark. No snow was falling.

"Down the hill," I said. "Over that way."

He shivered.

"Are you cold?" I said.

“No,” he said. “I don’t get cold.”

That was something my dad said when he was lying, when he was trying to pretend he was warm.

The streetlights were bright above us, sparkling through clear white glass. He did not touch me, but I knew he might. I knew it, and I knew what might happen, that I might fall into it, that I could, and I waited for it.

Acknowledgments

Thanks to the Ontario Arts Council, for their support of this project; to Barbara Berson, for reading with thoughtful enthusiasm; to Beverley Slopen, for betting on me; to my mother, for the gift of time; to Amanda, for her care of Angus and Annabella; and to Kevin, for all of the above.